BOOK 1 OF THE NEW A
FOR CHIL

Alice Parker's

Metamorphosis

Nicola Palmer

NICOLA PALMER

Alice Parker's Metamorphosis

2nd Edition published March 2012

First published December 2011

ALICE PARKER'S METAMORPHOSIS

For Alice, James and Lily

NICOLA PALMER

ALICE PARKER'S METAMORPHOSIS

Chapters

Chapter 1

A Secret Kidnapping

Alice Parker suddenly looked up from her homework. She leaped to her feet and peered out of the window in front of her desk, searching in the fading light of a December afternoon for what had caught her attention.

Nothing to be seen.

Again.

She sank down on to her chair with a frown and began to wonder if she was going mad. On several occasions recently, she thought she had seen someone passing by her window, which is ridiculous in itself, considering her bedroom is upstairs. But what made these experiences really peculiar was the fact that, when Alice looked carefully, there was no trace of movement in the garden, not even a bird flying past.

As if to check that she was normal, she glanced cautiously in the mirror on her wardrobe. Still wearing her school uniform, she had undone her burgundy and black striped tie and the top button of her shirt. Her woolly, grey tights had an unfortunate hole in the left knee. Long, unruly, blonde hair was at least in some sort of ponytail. Her face seemed the same as usual too, though the dark rings under her eyes were becoming quite prominent for a girl of thirteen. Perhaps it was lack of sleep making her mind play tricks on her. She did feel tired after all.

Nevertheless she decided to go out into the garden just to make sure. She opened her bedroom door and tripped over something very large, landing sprawled out with the stinging sensation of carpet burn on her hands. Groaning with annoyance, Alice picked herself up and saw the dog lying across her doorway.

'Stupid dog!' she grumbled. 'Why are you waiting here?'

Jack, an Irish Wolfhound the size of a small pony, wagged his tail and grinned.

'Come on, you silly old thing,' said Alice, irritated by his apparent amusement. 'We're going outside.'

Down in the kitchen she opened the back door. Jack paused on the step, sniffing the air.

'What's wrong with you now?' snapped Alice. 'Let me out, at least.' She pushed past him and wandered onto the patio. Just as she expected. The air was perfectly still, the branches of the trees motionless. There seemed to be nothing out of the ordinary in this sparse winter garden. Although, in this mysterious half-light, she felt a little uneasy as her grandad's words echoed in her mind. A few weeks ago, she had overheard a disturbing telephone conversation at his house.

'It's a dreadful dilemma,' she had heard him say in a low voice. 'I can't stop thinking about the poor fellow. Kidnapped in broad daylight, right under our noses.'

He hadn't mentioned it since and there had been nothing on the news about a missing person.

A rustling sound in some bushes made her jump. It turned out to be a squirrel digging frantically in leaves. 'Are you looking for something as well?' asked Alice, relieved.

The squirrel stopped momentarily to stare at her with its beady eyes, then carried on with its work. Alice could see her breath in the frosty air. Shivering, she turned to go back inside. But Jack had finally ventured out and was sniffing and licking the ground beneath the kitchen window. Crouching down beside him, Alice glimpsed something disappearing into his mouth.

'Drop it!' she shrieked, prizing his immense jaw open to retrieve it with her freezing fingers. It was a small piece of purple fabric, now glistening with slobber. Hardly worth getting excited about, but she put it in her pocket anyway. Disappointed, Alice trudged back up to her bedroom followed by the dog.

ALICE PARKER'S METAMORPHOSIS

It would be pointless asking the creature in the next room if he had seen anything from his window – the curtains were nearly always closed. Festering in his fusty lair, this nocturnal beast rarely emerged in the daytime, unless motivated by hunger or needing a lift back to university when the holidays were coming to an end. Alice suspected that all students of biochemistry were strange and her half-brother, Thomas, was no exception. She was rather envious of him since, although he was odd in every way, from his shoulder-length, curly hair, to the unusual smells that emanated from his room, he was popular. Oxford University suited him perfectly. Surrounded by other scientists who shared his weird interests, Thomas felt very much at home.

He and Alice had the same father. Mike Parker, a paramedic, was a tall man with thick, blonde hair and a kind face. He liked his food, and Alice sometimes wondered how he managed to run in an emergency, after eating the boxful of sandwiches he took to work. Thomas's mother died from an illness when he was a toddler, leaving his father to bring him up with a lot of help from his parents. Three years later, Mike met Alice's mum, Caroline, a local funeral director who had taken on her father's business. Petite with frizzy blonde hair and an equally bubbly personality, this lady had quite an effect on Mike and they married the following year. Alice came along shortly afterwards, providing Thomas with a subject for his pranks and jokes as they grew up.

5 o'clock. Her parents would be home soon and Alice would have to help prepare dinner, which had become quite complicated lately. Her mother had been encouraging the whole family to eat healthily, by which she meant vegetarian, experimenting with recipes involving obscure vegetables. Alice and Thomas didn't mind too much but their poor father was suffering from dreadful side effects in the evening and often slipped out of the room clutching his stomach. Alice

found it hugely entertaining to see the expression on his face when he returned.

The doorbell rang and Jack responded with his usual werewolf howl, followed by frenzied barking. Since nothing stirred in Thomas's room, Alice went to answer it. Looking out of the window on the landing, she saw Grandad Parker's ancient burgundy Morris parked outside. When she opened the door, he was standing on the step smiling. He was wearing his long, green oilskin coat which matched the colour of his eyes perfectly. His mop of wavy silver hair was poking out in a comical fashion beneath his flat cap, and he had what appeared to be a porridge oat stuck to his beard.

'I won't stop,' he announced. 'Your grandma asked me to drop these off for you.' He opened a large biscuit tin and showed Alice the homemade flapjacks inside.

'Ooh, thanks,' she said, taking the tin. 'They smell good!'

'Well, she thought you could do with a treat.'

Alice didn't ask why. She was already munching on a flapjack. 'Oh, I'm glad you're here,' she began with her mouth full.

'Is everything alright?' he asked, looking concerned.

'Yes, why wouldn't it be? Anyway, about that kidnapping you mentioned ...'

'SHHHHH!' hissed Grandad, looking all around to make sure they were alone.

Alice shut her mouth, taken aback by his response.

'Listen, you weren't meant to hear that conversation,' he whispered. 'So keep it to yourself. If the police get involved, the survival of that poor man as well as many others will be compromised. Understood?'

'Um ... well, no. If it's a secret, how come you know all about it?'

Perturbed by her questions, Grandad took a deep breath. 'I'm afraid I can't go into that now. It's complicated.'

Alice was getting frustrated. 'There must be *someone* who can help,' she said.

'Ah,' replied Grandad. 'Someone with a deep-rooted understanding of the situation. Someone unique, who belongs to his social circle as well as that of the kidnapper. Someone with backbone, who is prepared to take risks.'

'Well?'

'That someone doesn't exist.'

Alice sighed. She hated feeling helpless.

'I must dash,' said Grandad, looking at his watch. 'Don't worry yourself about this, we'll sort it soon enough.' He kissed her on the cheek and hurried off down the path.

We? What did he mean, *we*? Alice stared after him. Her grandad had always been an unpredictable character, but she had no idea what he was involved in this time. She closed the door, shrugged her shoulders and helped herself to another flapjack.

*

It was Friday evening and Alice's friend, Sarah, would be coming to stay the next day. Sarah Wiseman had what Alice considered a very normal life. In fact, if Sarah were not her best friend and a nice person, Alice would have found her irritating for being too perfect. Her family lived in a big house in the countryside and she had two sisters and two cats. They all got on wonderfully well – the three sisters often went clothes shopping together and, although aged thirteen, fifteen and eighteen, they all looked the same, with straight, shiny, chestnut hair and a pale, freckled complexion. Thomas referred to them as the Three Wise Men. At school their uniforms were immaculate. Their father had bought them each a leather briefcase, personalised with gold lettering and he even polished their shoes. Sarah and Sophie had been photographed for the school prospectus, carrying their briefcases and smiling, with their socks pulled up. Their older sister, Susan, had just spent her first term at Oxford but

Thomas said he hadn't seen her there. He was in his second year anyway.

Alice had never thought she was clever enough to go there. She was reasonably intelligent but wasn't one of those sickening people like Thomas, who could get brilliant marks without even trying. She had to make the effort. That is, until lately. Her marks had suddenly improved in all subjects. Dramatically. The strange part was that she hadn't been spending more time on her work. Her tiredness *was* due to lack of sleep, but not because she was staying up late.

*

After dinner Alice watched some TV and then went up to bed around 9.30pm. Jack lay down quietly next to her bed and she read a book for a while to try and relax. It wasn't long before she felt sleepy, since the book that Sarah had lent her was mind-numbingly boring. She had recommended it as 'fun and romantic' but Alice had already decided it was rubbish. Was this really what girls of her age enjoyed? She put it down and turned off her lamp.

First she lay on one side, then the other. She just couldn't get comfortable. After a while she lay on her front with her arms folded under her pillow and opened one eye to glance at her alarm clock. It was four minutes past eleven. This is how it had been for the last few weeks, being unable to get to sleep even though she felt tired. It was as if her body were deliberately trying to annoy her, creating aches and pains when she lay in bed, although she felt fine during the day. Every night she developed a mild headache with a sensation of pins and needles in her back and shoulders. Her father had suggested that she should improve her posture when sitting at her desk at school. Thomas had predicted that she was about to have an outbreak of spots on her back.

'Don't forget you'll need to squit them,' he added helpfully. Filled with horror, Alice had tried to study her back in the bathroom mirror, but, thankfully, nothing had appeared yet.

Having gazed at the old glow-stars on her bedroom ceiling for several hours and listened to the dog having a busy dream, she eventually fell asleep.

*

She was woken by her mother knocking on her bedroom door.

'Wake up, sleepy! Sarah will be here in half an hour. Your dad and I will give you a lift into town if you like.'

Alice dragged herself out of bed and into the shower. Although she'd managed a few hours sleep, she had the hangover feeling again. Not that she'd ever had a hangover, but had witnessed enough of Thomas's to be able to imagine how it felt – head spinning and not entirely sure if the world around you is real. Having taken a long shower trying to wake up properly, by the time she was dressed her father was sounding the horn outside. She raced downstairs and saw that Sarah was already waiting in the car with her parents. She joined her in the back seat.

'Morning, Brains!' said Sarah, smiling. Alice cringed. That was all she needed, her parents finding out what had been happening at school.

'Brains?' remarked her father, perplexed.

'You must be so proud of her, getting full marks for all her work lately,' Sarah rattled on. 'I just wish she'd stop showing me up. My mum and dad want to know why I can't do the same!'

'For pity's sake, shut up, Sarah,' snarled Alice, glaring at her.

'Alice!' her parents scolded her in unison. 'What's all this? Why on earth didn't you tell us how well you're doing? It's wonderful!' declared her mother. 'It must be my healthy cooking improving your brain power!'

Alice looked at her father's face in the rear view mirror. He rolled his eyes.

'Sorry,' whispered Sarah. 'I thought they knew. It's nothing to be ashamed of, anyway. I think it's brilliant, you lucky thing.'

Of course Sarah thought it was brilliant. She too had a sibling who was clever and a family who encouraged academic achievement. Shame most of the others at school didn't see things the same way. But enough of that until Monday. Alice was strong-minded – she pushed that thought aside and tried to look forward to the rest of the weekend.

Her father pulled in outside the entrance to the Priory Shopping Centre to drop them off.

'Treat yourselves to something nice,' insisted her mother and handed Alice a £10 note. 'That's for working so hard, you modest thing, you!'

'Er, thanks Mum,' said Alice. That was the problem, though. She hadn't worked hard at all, it just happened. Reluctantly putting the money into her pocket, she felt guilty as if she had cheated. They waved to her parents as they drove off.

'Listen, I really am sorry,' said Sarah. 'I didn't mean to drop you in it like that. Why keep it to yourself anyway?'

Alice sighed. 'I don't know. Maybe I don't want them to be disappointed if these results suddenly stop.'

'Why should they stop?'

Alice hung her head. More to the point, why had they started? 'Well, I haven't been feeling very well and I don't sleep much at the moment,' she admitted.

'I think you should take the weekend off. Don't do any homework – if Mrs Knight realises you haven't read your English chapters, just tell her you were ill.'

'Sounds like a plan!' agreed Alice. 'Fancy a large hot chocolate with the works?'

'Silly question!' laughed Sarah. 'I'm cold already!'

At The Coffee Cauldron, their favourite cafe, they were greeted by warmth and the aroma of sweet treats as they pushed the door open. Neither of them liked coffee, but they enjoyed the surroundings. They often came here for a drink and chocolate fudge cake on a Saturday. Sarah chose a comfy-looking sofa while Alice ordered two 'grande' hot chocolates with cream and marshmallows and two slices of cake. The usual lady behind the counter smiled at her. She was small with bright green eyes and always had her hair neatly covered with a patterned bandana.

'You look like you need this, my love,' she commented, grinning. 'It should do the trick. I'll bring them over to you.'

'Thanks,' said Alice and took her change.

Half an hour of lounging on a blue velvet sofa with silver cushions, over-indulging in sugar and chatting about Christmas presents really did make Alice feel better. She looked around the cafe at shelves stacked with tins of biscuits, jars of sweets and coffee beans and mugs of every description, all decorated with bright ribbons for Christmas.

'Only a few days of school until the holidays!' Sarah reminded her. 'I need to buy some Christmas cards, do you?'

Alice didn't feel like spreading festive cheer to anyone at school, but nodded her head and stood up to put on her coat and scarf. Bandana lady came to clear their table and whispered to Sarah,

'Take care of her, won't you? She's a special one,' nodding her head towards Alice, who had her back turned.

'Of course,' Sarah promised, slightly puzzled and ushered her 'special' friend outside.

After a couple of hours, they had had their fill of wandering from shop to shop in the cold, so walked home at a brisk pace to keep warm. Back at the house they went up to Alice's room, put on some music and leafed through the magazines they had bought. Alice wasn't really interested in girls' magazines, but bought one occasionally so that she could join in with conversations at school. She struggled to get excited about clothes and make-up. One of her secret hobbies was playing the harp. Unsurprisingly, that instrument wasn't taught at school and so she had a lesson at home once a week. Growing fruit and vegetables was her other passion - not that she could do much gardening at this time of year. She had never seen a magazine called 'Harpist's Weekly' or 'Vegetable Gardening for Girls,' and if she ever did, she would have to hide them from everyone at school to avoid being outcast completely. Imagine the reaction if they found out! 'What a freak, does she think she's an angel playing on a cloud?' and 'Dull old fart!' were just some of the comments she anticipated.

'Shall we watch one of the films you brought?' she asked Sarah, casting aside her 'Glitz' magazine.

'Sure, choose which one you like,' Sarah replied, rummaging in her bag. She handed over four DVDs and Alice turned the TV on. They just caught the news headlines:

'Bank robbers have escaped with a haul of over £300,000 – police are trying to determine how they accessed the main safe. Another lottery jackpot in lucky Warwickshire! The winner wishes to remain anonymous. And finally, a local entrepreneur has bought Aylesford Castle.'

Alright for some, thought Alice. She chose an animated film about monsters and they settled down on bean bags with the sweets they had bought earlier, Jack drooling at their feet.

The film was actually quite good, though the challenge lay in preventing Sarah from talking during the important bits. Each time she started to speak, Alice waved a jelly snake or fizzy cola bottle in front of her mouth.

When the film had finished, Alice went downstairs to let the dog out and fetch them a drink. Just as she was putting the orange juice back in the fridge, Jack started barking in the garden. She dashed outside to find him looking up at the sky, wagging his tail and barking.

'What's up boy?' she asked. 'Did you see a pigeon?' Jack loved chasing pigeons, the temptation of those fat, waddling birds was too much to resist, but they always managed to fly off before he could catch one. He grudgingly followed Alice back to the kitchen and she carried the drinks up to her room. Sarah was staring out of the window.

'What *on earth* was that?' she asked anxiously.

'What was what?'

'That thing that hovered outside your window just now! Jack must have seen it too, he was looking up here barking, I saw him down in the garden!'

'Er, a pigeon?' Alice felt butterflies in her stomach as she dared to hope that her friend had shared one of her strange experiences.

'That was no bird, it was something big.' Sarah had been reading with her back to the window when she noticed a shadow cast over her shoulder. She turned quickly and just glimpsed something darting away.

'Perhaps it was a pterodactyl,' joked Alice uneasily.

'Oh, very funny. You saw it as well, didn't you? I can tell by your face! What was it?'

Alice passed Sarah a drink and sat down on the bed. 'I didn't see anything. Not today.'

'You've seen it before?'

'I've seen *something* several times. I just don't know what it was, I didn't get a good look.'

'Well, I could swear it was a … no … it couldn't be. For a moment, I thought it was a person. Maybe it was a large bird after all, like a heron visiting your pond. Whatever it was, it gave me a fright.' She sat down next to Alice.

'I'm just glad you've seen it too,' admitted Alice, gulping down her orange juice. 'I began to think I was imagining things.'

After a take-away and plenty of dreadful Saturday night television, the girls went up to bed. Alice had a sofa-bed in her room which they made up for Sarah. For once, Alice was glad that her friend could talk the hind leg off a donkey. At least her whispering helped to pass the hour or two that she needed to fall asleep.

Unfortunately, that night, Sarah didn't sleep very well either. She remained wide awake, the vision outside the window that afternoon was playing on her mind. The concoction of junk food she had eaten probably wasn't helping either and she lay there listening to the dog snoring by Alice's bed. The room was light, as if the moon were trying to force open the curtains and she could see Jack's paws twitching as he was running along in his dream. Soon Alice began to fidget too and appeared to be fighting with her duvet. Sarah could hear her mumbling as well.

'What did you say, Alice? Are you OK?' she whispered, getting out of bed to see what was wrong.

Like a shot, Jack leaped to his feet and created a four-legged barrier between her and Alice, growling and baring his teeth.

Sarah stepped back, shocked. 'What's got into you?'

Jack put his front paws on the bed and licked Alice's face, whining. She grumbled, turned her back to them and went back to sleep, though the fidgeting and noises would continue all night. Jack resumed his position on the floor, keeping one eye on Sarah as she got back into bed. She had a rotten night and was justifiably grumpy the next morning.

It was quarter past ten when Alice finally woke up and Sarah was ready for her. She sat in her bed, arms folded, at a safe distance from Jack and demanded, 'Spill the beans then, what's going on with you and your nutty dog?'

As usual, Alice's head was spinning as she sat up. Great, an interrogation. She didn't like Sarah's snotty tone either, it was out of character. 'What do you mean?'

'First you toss and turn all night, making noises in your sleep. Then, when I get out of bed, your mad dog turns on me and snarls, as if I was going to hurt you. What with that thing outside the window yesterday, I'll be glad to go home.'

'Don't be like that, I'm sorry if I kept you awake but I can't help it. I told you I've not been sleeping very well. I get these pains and an itchy feeling across my back, then I get so hot and my head starts to hurt. She could feel the anger rising in her. 'You're sick of it after one night. Imagine how I feel! It's been going on for weeks. I've had enough!' she complained, thumping the bed with her fist in frustration.

'Well, what do your parents think? Your dad's a paramedic after all!'

'Nothing much. Dad thinks it could be bad posture causing backache and I don't bother mum with it. She's too busy with work at the moment. Plus, it's mostly during the night – it wouldn't go down too well if I woke them up with an itchy back and a headache would it?'

Sarah just shrugged and pulled a face that seemed to say, you're weird, I don't understand and I'm worried. 'You look awful as well,' she added.

'Thanks very much. I know. Anyway, let's get some breakfast, your mum will be here soon.'

At the kitchen table, without even realising it, Alice continued to unsettle her friend. Sarah watched in disbelief as she packed away a disturbing amount of food. Five slices of toast with lashings of apricot jam, two huge bowls of honey flakes and a whole carton of pineapple juice. She had noticed that Alice had been drinking a lot of fruit juice at school and assumed she was trying to be healthy. But this eating capacity was something different.

'You'll be sick if you're not careful,' she warned, 'and a fat porker.'

Alice put down her glass and looked guilty. 'I can't stop,' she confessed. 'I just want fruit and sugar all the time.'

She looked over her shoulder to make sure they were alone and lowered her voice. 'Mum thinks it's Thomas taking all this extra food and juice while he's home.' Her voice cracked as she added, 'but it's me.'

She put her head in her hands and dragged her fingers through her untidy hair, as if she wanted to tear it out. 'Please help me, Sarah, I don't know what's wrong with me and I'm so tired all the time.' She had begun to sniff as she was talking, and when she looked up, Sarah could see that tears were streaming down her cheeks.

'Course I will, if I can. Maybe you're just over-tired, as my mum says. Leave the homework and rest today. You'll feel better tomorrow and you won't look exhausted.'

Since her marks had been so impressive, Alice had taken a lot of stick from certain people at school. It was mainly jealousy, she knew that, but they had also been teasing her about yawning and the dark rings under her eyes. When Sarah left, she went back upstairs and lay on her bed. She reached for the book they were supposed to read for English by tomorrow, but after flicking from cover to cover, threw it down. Not a chance, she felt exhausted – perhaps Sarah was right. Still holding the piece of fabric she had intended to use as a bookmark, she now noticed how unusual it was. In spite of being rescued from the dog's mouth, it was beautifully shiny and soft. It sparkled with dazzling shades of purple as it reflected the light and as she ran it between her fingers, it felt cold on one side and warm on the other. Very odd. She fell asleep almost immediately. Now that really was odd.

Chapter 2

Brains and the Banana

Monday morning arrived and Alice awoke feeling surprisingly good. She had slept well and felt much better. No aches or itching, just a hot back and she could live with that. While her parents were still upstairs, she seized the opportunity to eat an enormous breakfast, stuffing more fruit and a carton of juice into her bag. She opened several cupboards in the hope of finding chocolate and spotted a pack of iced mince pies and a bag of red, white and green jelly beans on a high shelf. She turned to grab a chair so she could reach them.

'Would you like me to get those for you?'

The voice startled Alice. Thomas had crept downstairs and was standing in the kitchen doorway, watching her with a bemused expression.

'Er, I wanted something … for school, for the … er … Christmas fair,' garbled Alice.

'Well, we'd better get those down then, I think the kids will be disappointed with bananas and apple juice!'

Damn. He'd seen her take those as well. 'What are you doing up this early anyway?' she snapped. 'You don't usually leave your room during daylight hours in the holidays.'

'I love your charming manner in the morning,' he mocked. 'I'm catching a train to Oxford, I need some books from the library before Christmas. I'll walk to school with you. I was just leaving.'

He reached up to the top shelf and passed the Christmas goodies to Alice. She raised her eyebrows in approval as she realised that they were from The Coffee Cauldron. 'Actually, I did buy those for you,' he admitted.

'Oh! Sorry! Have I found my present then?' Alice felt guilty now.

'No, it's not your Christmas present, I just thought you might like them.'

Now she was flummoxed. Thomas being nice? Thoughtful, even. Something wasn't right.

'No need to thank me!' he said sarcastically, before she could think of a response. 'I've been taking the rap for all the food you've been eating, so I thought I'd get you some more, Wiglet!' Wiglet had been his nickname for her since they were small – it started when he meant to call her a wicked piglet for eating his Christmas selection pack one year. Alice smiled.

The walk to school began in silence, as she pondered why Thomas had indeed taken the blame for the missing food at home. As a rule, he would grass her up in an instant. She noticed that a blackbird and a robin seemed to be following them as they walked, flitting from tree to hedgerow, chirping happily. Perhaps everyone was simply in good spirits today. 'Thank you,' she murmured.

'For the sweets? No problem. Are you feeling alright today?' he asked.

Now this wasn't just unusual, this was downright strange. Now her brother appeared to care! 'What?' she exclaimed with a look of amazement.

'Well, you've not been yourself lately, have you? And anyone can see the bags under your eyes. This sleep thing, don't worry about it, it will right itself soon enough.'

Alice was confused but intrigued by his apparent awareness and concern. 'Have you had it as well?' she asked.

'Something very similar when I was your age. You'll grow out of it.'

'I feel fine today anyway,' Alice assured him. 'And a hot back in this weather is a bonus!'

'Oh ... er ... how convenient!' replied Thomas. They carried on walking, their faces glowing in the wintery air, until they came to Beaumont Avenue. Langley School was a beautiful old building, a former manor house converted into a private school, with two town houses opposite forming the infant school and sixth form centre. Alice had been a pupil there since she was four years old.

'Have a good day then, Wiglet,' said Thomas with a grin.

'Er, thanks, you too,' muttered Alice and watched him carry on down the road towards the station. How bizarre, she thought, as she stood at the entrance. Not just Thomas's behaviour, but those two birds had now stopped and were looking down at her from the tree by the school gate. 'Well, that makes a change, it seems everyone wants my company this morning,' she concluded before turning to walk up the steps.

She spoke too soon. As she hurried up the grand staircase to her classroom, she was pushed against the wall as the coven jostled past her, looking down their noses at her as if she had stepped in dog poo and brought it in onto the carpet. The coven comprised Lucinda Rowbottom, Katy Blackwell and Olivia Staines-Downe, and Alice despised all three. They were at the centre of the 'cool crowd,' which, needless to say, Alice had never been part of. Lucinda No-Bottom was a tall, thin girl with pale blue eyes and long, brown hair. She would have been quite pretty if it weren't for those ears which stuck out beneath her hair and reminded Alice of a chimpanzee. She was a horsey type with several ponies of her own. Her father was a formidable, insufferable man, a multi-millionaire making his money from several different businesses. A finger in every pie, as Grandad called it. Brian Rowbottom was feared by some and loathed by many, renowned for stopping at nothing to get what he wanted. Money was at the centre of his world; he wanted to take over everything, it seemed. No wonder Lucinda was so obnoxious. Katy Smackwell had no pony of her own, which was probably why she followed Lucinda everywhere like a bad smell. She was short and blonde, with an equally short modern haircut. It was shaved into a deep V in her neck, which Alice thought made her look evil. Olivia Stains-Brown was, unfortunately, stunning. She was like a catwalk model, with a perfect figure and shoulder-length ebony hair. All the girls envied her, though some took comfort in her one weakness – she was painfully stupid.

Alice sighed and carried on up to Room 12, the form room of Year 8. Spaced around this elegant landing with its ornate wooden balustrade, were five classrooms and to the right, the headmistress's office. Unfortunately for Alice's class, this was next to Room 12. As she neared the door to her form room, she saw Sebastian Seaton standing in his usual place outside the door. He rather fancied himself as a comedian and often nominated himself as doorman. It was school tradition that someone would stand outside to greet the teacher, but also provided the opportunity for that pupil to bang on the door on their approach, warning everyone to shut up and look sharp. For Sebastian it was the chance to practise his stand-up comedy on all who entered, making a witty or cruel remark, depending on who you were. This morning for Alice, he simply pulled down his eyes to reveal the red, bloodshot part, then yawned 'Sorry to drag you out of bed.'

She pursed her lips and waited as he opened the door, waving his hand in a grand gesture. 'I can see you as a toilet attendant rather than a comedian,' she said as she walked in. He pulled a face like a sad clown and darted back outside. The room was noisy with friends chattering and laughing about their weekend. Sarah was waiting for her in their usual place, second row from the back, but Alice had to walk past the coven to reach her.

'Nice tights,' said Lucinda No-Bottom, pointing a bony finger at the hole in the left knee. Quinton O'Connor looked over and wolf-whistled.

'Won't Mummy buy you some new ones for doing so well?' he asked with a grin. His sidekick, Lawrence Lovett, sniggered, while trying to extract a chewy sweet from his brace with his finger.

'Want this?' asked Alice sarcastically. She waved the window pole in front of him, which had a large brass hook on the end. Lawrence shut his mouth and went red.

Sarah was laughing, but soon stopped when she realised that Alice wasn't. 'So? Did you get some rest yesterday?' she asked, changing the subject.

'Yes, thanks. I had a much better night's sleep too.'

There was a frantic banging at the classroom door as Sebastian alerted them in his usual, subtle manner to the arrival of Mrs Barnett, their form mistress. They fell silent and stood up when she entered the room.

'Good morning Year 8!' she beamed.

'Good morning Mrs Barnett,' they droned in reply, like bored infants at a pantomime. They sat down, scraping their chairs and shuffling in their seats as Mrs Barnett called the register and read out some announcements. Over the heads in front of her, all Alice could ever see was a talking mass of red curls at the front desk. She had the most wild, curly hair, which she attempted to tame with combs and clips, but by the end of the school day it had usually broken free, making her look as though her pupils had dragged her through a hedge. At 9 o'clock the buzzer sounded for first lesson.

'Enjoy maths!' she said and dashed off.

'Is she trying to be funny?' asked Quinton, pulling out his maths textbook and beating himself over the head with it in slow motion. He hated maths and they had a double lesson on Monday mornings. Alice tried to look sympathetic, though it wasn't very convincing.

'Ooh, test results today!' remembered Sarah. 'Bet you've done well.'

'If I have I'll be amazed. I didn't even revise I was so tired.' Towards the end of term, there was always a maths test on everything they had learned that term, which was quite a lot. It had taken place on Thursday and Alice had felt so rotten last week that she just didn't feel up to revising.

'So you say,' Sarah sneered.

'I wrote what I could on the day and that's it,' protested Alice. 'My dad says not to worry as long you answer every question.' And she had, with time to spare, which she found disturbing.

Announced by a thump on the door, Mrs Myers walked in briskly, waving her hand in an impatient gesture telling the class to sit down before they could say a word. Unnerved, they looked at each other anxiously.

'Oh dear,' sighed Sarah.

'Well, everyone, we can safely say that wasn't your greatest performance. I take it you haven't enjoyed algebra this term?' she asked menacingly, in her lilting Welsh accent. After no reply from the roomful of pupils fidgeting uneasily in their chairs, she continued regardless.

'Results in the usual manner, read out according to the register.'

They all hated this, some hid their faces behind their books. Their marks were revealed with groans and grimaces. For once, no one had more than 65% and that was Julia Hunt, the maths genius. Alice was red-faced and panicked. Her name had not been called – had she been left out for a reason, was her mark that bad?

'Have I missed anyone?' asked Mrs Myers.

'Er, just me,' said Alice quietly, her hand only half raised as if she were expecting it to be bitten off.

'Oh, yes, yours …' She smiled and held her clipboard to her chest. 'Alice Parker 100%.'

A brief, stunned silence was followed by an outburst of noise, exclamations of amazement and disgust, one or two congratulatory comments and Lawrence attempting to stick his fingers down his throat and be sick. Quinton lifted the lid of his desk and pretended to be Alice, a mock-look of surprise on his face like that of a winning beauty queen, bowing to left and right, then blowing kisses in the direction of Mrs Myers. The coven had turned around and was looking at her scornfully, shaking its three heads. Even Sarah looked as though she had been slapped in the face by an invisible hand, her mouth partly open ready to say something, but seemingly unable to get the words out. Alice had her crimson face in her hands, elbows on her desk. She was absolutely horrified. How could this happen? She had only ever been average at maths and now this, even without revision?

'Don't be embarrassed Alice,' said Mrs Myers calmly. 'We're all over the moon for you. You should be proud of yourself, you've clearly worked hard for this.'

Alice cringed and wished the floor beneath her chair would open and swallow her up. She glanced cautiously at Sarah, who finally managed to release the words that had been stuck in her throat.

'Well done. You are a brain box, aren't you?'

'I just can't believe it,' whispered Alice. 'I don't know what to say.'

'Anyway, Year 8,' Mrs Myers continued. 'Now that someone has set a precedent for what *can* be achieved when you put your mind to it, let's start the next chapter. Circles, arcs and sectors for the last week of term.'

There was a widespread moan and a voice from the front piped up, 'Can we make the circles into Christmas baubles, Miss?'

'Grow up, Sebastian,' she snapped.

When the buzzer finally rang for break, Alice had never been so relieved. She packed her rucksack as quickly as she could and rushed off without waiting for Sarah. She headed for a dark corner of the locker room, where she tried to pull herself together and munched thoughtfully on the jelly beans that Thomas had bought for her.

'Only art and English to get through now,' she whispered aloud, giving herself a pep-talk. 'No marks or test results due.' She sank back into some coats hanging on pegs and reached into her bag for the mince pies.

*

Alice looked forward to art. She considered the lessons a fun part of her timetable. They didn't even have to stand up for the teacher – Mr Sheldon was always there already, enjoying life in his light, airy art room. Alice had wondered if his hair and beard were white because the sunlight in there had bleached them, he spent so much time there. The class sat around two huge tables, which had been prepared with a neatly arranged bowl of fruit at each end. Sarah threw down her bag on the chair next to Alice.

'And where did you get to at break?' she demanded, sounding miffed.

'Can I have your attention, please,' began Mr Sheldon in his usual, quiet manner. Alice was grateful for the interruption. They settled down.

'No prize for guessing what you will be drawing today,' he said with a grin. 'The purpose of this exercise is to study the shape of the objects, notice where the light falls and where the shadows are cast. Paper and charcoal will be passed round by Sebastian and Julia, please.' They got up to do as asked. 'And before any prankster considers it – DO NOT TOUCH THE FRUIT! This is a still life exercise – it's called *still* life for a reason.'

Sebastian knew that was aimed at him and turned his nose up. 'This paper smells like sick,' he informed everyone as he handed it out. He had a point.

Alice set to work immediately, hoping that the look of concentration on her face would deter Sarah from asking any more questions. It worked. She soon had the outline of the fruit piled in its bowl on her paper and prepared to draw each item in detail. Starting with the orange on top, she drew the fruit carefully but quickly, adding shading to each piece as she completed it. Several times she tried to chew the end of the charcoal. It was a bad habit, chewing pens and pencils when she was focussed on something. She even drew the shadow cast by the whole bowl upon the table. When she had finished she sat back and assessed her work. 'Not bad,' she thought. She looked around to see how everyone else was doing and, to her surprise, they hadn't accomplished much. Sarah was still drawing the outline, Quinton and Lawrence were painstakingly putting dots on the first orange to convey its texture.

Fortunately, no one had noticed that Alice had finished. She could feel the colour rising in her cheeks as she began to panic – the last thing she wanted to do was draw attention to herself again. She leaned forward positioning her left arm around her work, adding a few tiny strokes to make it look as though she were still working. She stared blankly at the fruit. After a couple of minutes time-wasting, the smell of the fruit seemed so strong to her, it was almost overwhelming. She licked her lips. It did look good. Her mouth watered at the thought of the juicy orange, or better still, that slightly speckled, over-ripe banana. Without realising, she had begun to rock backwards and forwards in her chair, overcome by desperation for sugar and fear of what was now inevitable …

She lunged across the table and seized the banana, tearing it open and eating great chunks of it as fast as she could. It was so sweet, she felt happier with every bite. Immersed in the pleasure of consuming her prey, Alice was oblivious to the shrieks and cries of annoyance that erupted from her classmates. Mr Sheldon stood at the far end of their table, arms folded, shaking his head.

Sarah thumped the table in temper and bellowed, 'ALICE!' in her face.

Alice blinked several times, looking around with a dazed expression. One by one, she saw the furious faces of those who had been drawing the same bowl as herself, then the amusement of the rest of the class. Looking down at the banana skin in her hand, the reality of what she had just done sank in. She felt a tear run down her burning red face and wiped it briskly with the sleeve of her jumper.

'I'm sorry everyone,' she said, her voice trembling. 'I don't know what came over me.'

'Perhaps hunger got the better of you,' suggested Mr Sheldon. 'Make sure you're eating enough, Alice.'

Sarah snorted and turned her face away. 'No fear,' she muttered. Alice hung her head in shame.

'There's another banana here,' said Mr Sheldon. 'Julia, would you attempt to rearrange the fruit as it was, please. The rest of you, back to work, the show's over.' He leaned over Alice's shoulder and studied what she had drawn.

'That's actually your best piece of work yet. Pretty good, considering we're only twenty-five minutes into the lesson. Have a go at something else.' He reached up to one of his many shelves of arty junk and chose another object which he placed in front of her. It appeared to be a dog's skull. Nice.

'Rover will keep an eye on you for the rest of the lesson,' whispered Quinton with a smirk. Alice had already noticed that it did, indeed, have one bony eye socket on her and one on the fruit bowl.

*

Lunch passed without incident, thankfully, apart from the predictable mockery over the banana episode. As they queued in the canteen, Alice daren't even look at the desserts, as she could hear muffled giggling and chuckling behind her.

'Just ignore them,' said Sarah. She seemed to have forgotten her annoyance earlier. Alice chose a jacket potato with baked beans and a carton of orange juice. She slid her tray reluctantly to the cashier, grumpy because she had deprived herself of pudding, but as she reached this rather rotund, jolly dinner lady, a bowl of apple crumble was pushed onto her tray.

'There you go, my dear,' she said kindly. 'That's on me.'

'Really?' queried Alice, surprised but very pleased. 'Thank you very much.' She paid for the rest and hurried off to find a spot for her and Sarah at a table away from their year.

'I take it you want to eat in peace,' commented Sarah. Alice nodded. She tucked in to her potato, making a conscious effort to slow down, although she was impatient to start the crumble.

'Please tell me you didn't read the chapters for English,' said Sarah, 'because I didn't.'

'No, I didn't. I flicked through the book and thought I'd better do as you told me, so I put it down and went to sleep. In the same way as I didn't revise for that flippin' maths test. I promise.'

'Oh, great. In that case, I expect you know the book inside out,' groaned Sarah, chasing her lumpy soup around the bowl.

'I don't see how.'

'Nothing would surprise me with you at the moment.'

They finished their lunch in silence, both dreading the next lesson, though for very different reasons.

Their fears were justified. As Mrs Knight chose people at random to summarise those chapters they had read, Sarah was found out. She clearly hadn't read her three and stuttered her excuses shame-facedly. She was given another four to read by Wednesday. Alice was also picked on, in spite of trying to hide behind Olivia, but as she opened her mouth to confess that she too had not done her homework, an impressive account of her chapters flowed out. Only when it had finished could she slam her mouth shut like a trapdoor.

'Where did that come from?' she asked herself, flabbergasted.

'You shocking liar,' hissed Sarah, furious.

'Excellent, Alice,' observed Mrs Knight. 'A commendable précis.'

As soon as she turned her back to write on the blackboard, Lucinda spun round in her seat. Twisting her ponytail, she had made a bun on her head like Mrs Knight's and was blowing kisses at Alice. Even Sarah couldn't help smiling at this.

'Charming,' said Alice. 'I'm telling you, I never read it.'

'You must be possessed then, since you've no control over your tongue,' Sarah pointed out.

'Un ... be ... lievable! Do you honestly think ...' Alice began to rant.

'No, not really. You're just a lucky cow, being brainy and not working for it.'

'Quiet girls,' barked Mrs Knight. 'Unless you want more chapters.'

*

After a slow walk home, contemplating her bewildering day, Alice opened the front door to be greeted by Jack, who had been waiting for her. Barking and wagging his tail, he jumped up and licked her face, towering above her on his hind legs.

'Hello boy,' said Alice, dropping her rucksack to give him a hug. 'At least someone still likes me.'

Thomas appeared at the top of the stairs. 'That good, was it?'

'Yep.' She wandered into the kitchen followed closely by Jack, took a carton of apple juice from the fridge and skulked up to her room. She threw herself down on the bed and stared at the ceiling. Why did she have to be different? Would she never fit in?

There was a knock at the door and Thomas came in with a packet of Jammy Dunkers.

'What happened?' he asked, offering her a biscuit.

'Why do you care, all of a sudden?' snapped Alice defensively.

Thomas raised his hands in defeat and retreated to the door. 'Only asking, grumpy.'

'You can leave the biscuits.'

'Yes m'lady.' He put them on her desk and tiptoed out backwards.

'Weirdo.'

'I heard that.'

She thought it was strange that he was spending less time in his room lately and more time sticking his nose into what she was doing. More to the point, what wasn't strange at the moment. Hardly sleeping, aches and pains, eating loads, suddenly doing well at school and even knowing the content of a book she hadn't read. Not to mention the visions outside her window, or the secret kidnapping that Grandad knew about. And now Thomas being nice to her! Where he was concerned, being normal wasn't normal.

For Alice, that night proved as rotten as the day had been. Wide awake, she was turning things over and over in her mind, searching in vain for answers. Then came the usual headache followed by a hot, itchy back. Only tonight it was worse. Far worse. There was a deep pain in her upper back and shoulders as well as the itching. No matter what she did, she couldn't get comfortable. At ten past two in the morning, she couldn't stand it any longer and went for a shower. Holding the cool jet of water on her back she breathed deeply as it brought relief to the soreness. She stayed there for twenty minutes or so, then wrapped a towel around herself to return to her room. But first she turned her throbbing back to the mirror and craned her neck to look over her shoulder. It seemed rather swollen and the skin was very red and angry-looking.

'Please, no!' she gasped. 'I don't want my back to be as spotty as Richard Pickel's face!' Anxious and dismayed, she tiptoed across the landing.

'Pssst.'

Alice jumped, startled, and saw Thomas's head poking out from his bedroom door.

'What's up?' he asked in a low voice.

'Just my back playing up again,' she replied, trying to sound brave.

'Wait a sec,' he said, disappearing into his room. He came back with a small, royal-blue glass bottle. 'Spray some of this on before you get back into bed. It's really good.'

'What is it?'

'Just something I was given by a friend, for skin problems.'

'Okaaaay,' agreed Alice reluctantly. She took it and closed her door.

The antique-looking bottle may have looked suspicious, but since the itching had started again, Alice sprayed plenty on. 'Worth a try,' she muttered to herself. To her surprise, her skin instantly felt calmer and the pain subsided. Finally! She got back into bed and fell asleep.

Chapter 3

The Metamorphosis

'So, how was the spot spray?' asked Thomas.

'Very funny,' said Alice, as she stood up from the kitchen table after another mammoth breakfast. 'Actually, it was really good. There aren't any spots yet though, just redness.'

'Well, that's something. Can you do me a favour and post this in the first letter box you pass this morning? It's urgent.' He handed her a small envelope addressed to a Dr. I. Darnell of Oak Tree Way, Wipfin Village.

'Will do,' she said. There had been a sprinkling of snow during the night, so Alice put on her winter blazer, scarf and gloves. She wiggled her arms backwards and forwards, finding her coat a little tighter than usual, but shrugged her shoulders and stuffed the envelope into her pocket. Perhaps all the extra food was catching up with her. She'd have to be more careful.

After a few minutes of brisk walking in the snow, she noticed that the same two birds as yesterday seemed to be following her again. At the end of the road she saw a letterbox next to a tree and dropped in Thomas's letter.

'Funny, I don't remember that box being there before,' she said to the two birds, who were now sitting on top of it. The birds looked at each other, then flew off, chirping loudly.

Alice continued on her way. On the other side of the road she spotted a group from her class outside the newsagents. They were looking in her direction, laughing. Richard Pickel waved a banana above his head, calling her name and whistling her like a dog. Enraged, Alice saw a gap in the traffic and charged across the road. She stormed over to Pickel and snatched the banana. Pointing rudely at the mass of bulging, puss-filled spots on his chin, she blurted out,

'Looks like you've got plenty of custard to go with this.' Head held high, she walked away, but quickened her pace before anyone else could mock her in the street. Shrieks of mirth could be heard from the group she left behind as Pickel became their new verbal punch-bag. She felt a bit cruel and lowered her head, which caused her nearly to collide with someone as she turned the corner. It was bandana lady from The Coffee Cauldron.

'Ooh, slow down! Oh, morning love, how are you today?' she asked.

'Er, fine thanks,' mumbled Alice, hardly lifting her head and hurried on. Bandana lady wrinkled her brow in concern and paused on the corner for a moment, watching as Alice scuttled away.

Once inside the school entrance, Alice dashed up the stairs, but hesitated at the top, dreading her welcoming comment from Sebastian. To her relief, as she looked over towards her form room, she saw that Sarah was standing with him. She waved and beckoned Alice over. Sebastian stood aside looking disappointed, his arms folded. '*I* was going to give you that,' he stressed, nodding towards a banana that Sarah had attempted to hide up her sleeve.

'How long did it take you to think of that one?' asked Alice, forcing a smile.

'Thanks, Sarah,' she whispered as they walked to their seats.

'No problem. I've got something for you as well, to make up for yesterday. I wasn't very nice, was I? Anyway, I thought you'd like these.' She handed Alice a small, but heavy, white paper bag. It was full of coloured jellies, large ones in the shape of fruit, coated in sugar. Alice beamed.

'Thanks!' She lifted the lid of her desk to hide and started scoffing them hungrily. While she was eating, she had a familiar sensation. Similar to the fruit bowl experience yesterday, but now the whole room smelled incredibly strong.

She could smell bad things, like sweaty socks and identify which individual it was coming from, but also pleasant smells. 'Can you smell strawberry jam?' she asked Sarah.

'What? No! Just your sweets.'

'It's not that. There's a really strong smell of strawberries.' She sniffed the air, concentrating like a sniffer dog. 'Julia, are you wearing strawberry perfume?' she asked.

Julia, who sat two rows in front of them, turned around. 'No, I'm not,' she replied, blushing. 'I have got strawberry jam sandwiches in my lunchbox though.' She tapped her bag, as if to prove their existence.

'Oh, sorry,' said Alice, shame-faced. She wished she had bitten her lip – now she'd done it again, drawn attention to herself.

'Incredible! You freak me out more each day!' said Sarah.

'Can you smell me, Alice?' called the squeaky voice of Lawrence, sniggering across the gangway.

'Always. And today, stronger than ever. I'd say you're rotten.' His face fell. She heard him whisper to Quinton,

'Do you think I've left an old egg roll in my desk?'

Alice vowed that she would not show herself up again that day. And she managed it, though she did start to feel ill during the last lesson. Although she made it through history, she really struggled with the walk home. Luckily, Sarah was with her. She always went home with Alice on a Tuesday while her sister had orchestra practice after school.

As she shuffled up Albany Road, Sarah carrying her rucksack, she admitted, 'I feel dreadful. I'm so dizzy and my back's killing me.' Sarah took her arm to support her but just as they reached Alice's gate, she collapsed.

'ALICE!' screamed Sarah, dropping to her knees in the snow. The front door flew open and Thomas ran towards them carrying a blanket. He sat his sister up, put the blanket around her shoulders and carried her inside. Sarah ran after him, crying, while Jack was barking frantically, darting around in distress.

'Is she alright, what's wrong with her?' sobbed Sarah.

'She'll be fine, soak this in water,' he commanded and he lay Alice in the recovery position on the kitchen floor. As Sarah handed him the drenched blanket, she saw movement in the back of Alice's blazer.

'WHAT'S THAT?' she shrieked.

'Grab those scissors,' dictated Thomas, pointing, and carefully rolled Alice on to her front.

He swiftly cut a line up the back of her blazer. Even through her shirt they could see that her upper back was grossly swollen. They were clearly just in time as, at that moment, something erupted from Alice's back and ripped through her shirt. It was large, glistening with moisture, though not a speck of blood. As it expanded outside her body, rising up into the air, it suddenly seemed to fall in half. Sarah screamed. It wasn't one thing, it was two. Two … wings.

It proved too much for Sarah. Thomas now had a pool of her vomit to deal with.

'Fantastic,' he groaned.

*

Fifteen silent minutes later, Alice was sitting up drinking pineapple juice, the wet blanket draped around her. She looked dreadful. Sarah was sitting on the floor too, though at a safe distance from her friend, her back against a cupboard. She was petrified and bewildered. What she had just witnessed happening to her friend was terrifying, like something from a horror film. Yet Thomas knew exactly what to do and had behaved as though it were perfectly normal. Finally, she whispered,

'Thomas … why?'

He looked at her, anxiously rubbing his sister's hand, unsure what to tell her.

'Yes Thomas, why?' murmured an exhausted Alice. 'Why me? And how did you know what to do?'

Thomas took a couple of deep breaths.

'Sarah, I'm trusting you, as Alice's friend, to keep this to yourself. If you open your mouth, you will be putting many people at risk. Do you understand?'

She nodded. Those words sounded strangely familiar to Alice.

'Well, it's hereditary,' he began. 'I'm one, Grandad Parker is one, though it skipped a generation so Dad isn't.'

'One what?' asked Alice, wide-eyed.

'Finwip. That is, a Fully Integrated Winged Person. That's what we've named ourselves, anyway. Over hundreds of years, winged people have evolved to adapt to modern society. I mean, we live as normal people with our wings and abilities hidden. Grandad never even told Dad, he only told me when I went through this a few years ago. Luckily, he recognised the signs and made sure I was with him when it happened.'

'And how do I hide *these* monsters?' asked Alice, alluding to her wings. 'I haven't seen them properly, but I can tell that they're enormous.'

'Don't worry. When you're calm, they'll go back in of their own accord and it won't hurt at all. But remember you will always have a mark on your back, a dark line which is where they emerge from. You'll need to be careful and keep your back hidden when you get changed at school. And at home – we're not telling Mum and Dad. Grandad doesn't think it would be a good idea.'

Alice sighed, trying to take it all in. So Grandad was a Finwip. She felt sure that must be linked to the secret kidnapping. 'What did you mean by *abilities*?' she suddenly remembered.

'We each have special abilities. I mean, skills that are enhanced compared with normal humans. It seems you're going to be super-intelligent.'

'She already is,' said Sarah quietly. She was beginning to feel better, at least things were starting to make sense now.

'What's your ability?' asked Alice.

'If I'm honest, they don't know yet,' said Thomas. 'Some abilities take longer to develop than others. They think it will be something to do with science, so perhaps uni is the best place for me at the moment.'

'*They?*'

'The rest of our people. Our local group, anyway. You'll have to meet them soon, they've been very worried about you.'

Alice stroked Jack, who was lying next to her. She half expected him to turn into a frog, everything seemed so ridiculous. If it weren't for the sinister mound beneath the blanket around her shoulders and the unmistakable smell of sick in the air, she would have sworn she was dreaming.

'Is this why I've been eating so much?' she asked Thomas.

'Oh yes,' he said, smiling. 'Developing wing discs requires a great deal of nutrients. And yours look like butterfly wings, so your symptoms of craving fruit and sugar were completely normal. You know, as a butterfly feeds on nectar.'

'There are different sorts? What sort are your wings?'

'Dragonfly,' he replied in a matter-of-fact manner. He had a peek at her wings under the blanket. 'Come on, I'll help you stand up. We've kept them moist to give you a chance to recover, but now we need to let them dry off. They can take one to three hours to inflate properly and get the blood circulating. On your feet, Sarah, we'll help her up to her room and open the window.'

She scrambled to her feet and put on a brave face. Squeezing Alice's hand, she and Thomas supported her under each arm and struggled up the stairs. Sarah kept looking over her shoulder and then leaning forwards, as though she feared that if the wings touched her, the condition might be contagious. They sat Alice sideways on her chair, since the backrest would be in the way of her wings, and Thomas flung the window wide open. Then he carefully released her wings from the blanket.

Alice turned her head to look at herself in the mirror and stared in fear at her hideous wings. They didn't look like butterfly wings to her. They were dark and menacing, towering above her shoulders and almost touching the floor as she sat on the chair. At first glance, she reminded herself of one of those eerie stone angels you find in a cemetery. She shivered and a tear ran down her ashen face.

As the cold air blew in, her wings started to dry and become more transparent. Sitting on the bed, Thomas and Sarah watched as they became beautifully shiny and clearly shaped like those of a butterfly. There was no denying they were huge, though.

Thomas offered his hand and Alice stood up cautiously.

'I feel a bit wobbly,' she complained. 'They feel so strange.'

'That's because they're still damp,' said Thomas. 'After a while, you get used to it. Never slouch, though, you need to stand tall with those wings.'

'Surely they're too big for me?' moaned Alice. She turned this way and that, trying get a better view in the mirror, as if trying on a new outfit.

'Not at all,' Thomas assured her. 'In fact, you could be one of the lucky few. You might be able to fly.'

'WHAT?!' Alice raised her voice.

'Most of us can't fly because we have evolved that way. We don't need to and anyway, we can't in front of people. But some, who have exceptionally large wings in relation to their body, can fly a little.'

Alice shook her head in disbelief. Sarah had now lost all fear and was just plain jealous. She looked up at the window.

'Thomas,' she asked, 'do you know what we saw hovering outside on Saturday?'

'Not just on Saturday,' added Alice.

'Yes, it was Imogen. She's the leader of our community and has been keeping an eye on you. She knew your metamorphosis was imminent and was concerned about your health.'

'Mmm,' grunted Alice. 'Well, I suppose that's good news. I thought I was going to be kidnapped.'

Thomas seemed baffled – he obviously had no idea what she was referring to. 'You've had a rough time,' he said. 'But you've got a darn fine pair of wings, you lucky thing!'

Alice looked away and noticed the time on the clock. 'Oh no, Sarah, your mum will be here in a few minutes!'

Sarah was mortified.

'Stay calm,' insisted Thomas. 'Alice, you need to stay up here and get some rest. Sarah and I will go downstairs and tell her mother that *you* were sick when you got home. We'll have to continue that story anyway for school tomorrow. You won't be going in.'

'What do we tell Mum and Dad?'

'Dad's on late shift today. I'll tell Mum you've been ill and want to get some sleep. That way, she'll leave you in peace and phone school for you tomorrow as well. Don't worry, I'll bring you some food later.'

'You've got it all under control, haven't you?' said Alice, relieved.

'I've had plenty of time to plan for it,' said Thomas. 'Thank goodness it was during my holidays.'

'Bye then, Alice,' said Sarah, standing up to go. 'I hope you're going to be OK. Give me a call if you can.' She felt, given the circumstances, that she should give her friend a hug, but much as she wanted to comfort her, she didn't want to touch those wings at any price. Alice sensed her reticence.

'It's OK,' she said. 'Thank you. You've been great.'

Thomas closed the door and led Sarah downstairs. 'You did well, kid,' he said with a grin. 'Not sure we'll ever get rid of that smell in the kitchen, though.'

*

Alice awoke to find she still had wings. When she tried to turn over she realised there was something in the way. For an instant, she thought it had been a vivid nightmare. Now the reality was starting to set in.

'Nope, it's true,' she muttered to herself. 'I am officially a freak.' She sighed and Jack stood up from his favourite spot next to her bed, where he had been guarding her all night. He was smiling as usual. 'It's all right for you,' said Alice, reaching up to stroke his head. 'Your life's simple. I don't even know how to get out of bed today.'

After a moment's thought she rolled on to her front and moved slowly into a kneeling position. Then she stepped carefully off her bed. Jack retreated a couple of paces, as if perturbed by what his owner had become.

'Please don't be afraid,' whispered Alice. 'I'm still me, even with these horrid things on my back.'

He plodded back and licked her hand. She was still wearing the damp blanket from the previous afternoon. 'I suppose this is all that will fit me at the moment,' she said to Jack. 'Not exactly fashionable, what would the coven say if they saw me in this?'

'I think your outfit would be the least of their worries if they could see you right now,' said a voice outside her bedroom door.

Alice turned the key to let Thomas in and stood behind the door to hide.

'It's OK,' he said. 'Mum's already left for work and she phoned the school for you. Dad's asleep. I told them you've got an upset stomach.'

'I've got an upset body.'

'Exactly! Not much of a fib, was it? Besides, you can do no wrong at the moment as top of the class!'

Alice scowled.

'Time's getting on, you need to get dressed – places to go, people to see.'

'People?'

'OK, Finwips then.'

'And what am I supposed to wear?'

'It doesn't matter. Your clothing dilemma will be solved when we get there. Hurry up.' He closed the door as he left.

Great, thought Alice, opening her wardrobe. She chose a yellow shirt and put it on back to front, only fastening the lowest buttons beneath her wings. She felt as if she were wearing a toddler's art overall, with jeans and winter boots. Even brushing her hair was a challenge, as the upper part of her wings got in the way. She left it in a ponytail, dangling between them, threw the blanket over her wings and pulled it around herself like a cloak. She crept downstairs without disturbing her father and found Thomas waiting in the hallway. He was grinning.

'You look like the Hunchback of Notre Dame.'

'Shut up and help me put this cardigan on back to front,' she snapped, reaching for her school one on the peg. 'What about breakfast?' she asked as Thomas did up the buttons behind her.

'We'll be well looked after where we're going,' he replied.

'Where *are* we going?'

'You'll see soon enough.' He put the blanket back around her and ushered her out of the door.

As they walked down Albany Road, the snow crunching beneath their feet, Alice felt terribly self-conscious and kept her head down. 'Is anyone looking at me?' she asked Thomas.

'Relax, there's no one around. Lucky for you it's winter and you can cover up. You would look an idiot wearing that blanket-cloak in August!'

They reached the new letterbox next to the giant oak tree. Thomas stopped and looked all around, making sure the coast was clear.

'Now watch carefully and follow me,' he instructed. He placed his hand inside the letterbox for a moment, palm upwards, then Alice heard a strange grating sound. A door slid open in the immense trunk of the oak tree. Alice's jaw dropped, but before she could say anything, Thomas stepped inside and pulled her in. The door closed behind them.

Inside it was dark and smelled damp. There were tiny specks of light glowing in the wall, but not sufficient to put Alice at ease. She had pretended to take yesterday's events in her stride, but now she was really feeling the strain.

'I don't like this at all,' she whined. 'There's not much room in here.'

'Shhh, it's only for a minute. Hold tight.' Thomas guided her hand to a rail and they started to travel downwards.

'Oh no, what next?' groaned Alice, holding on for dear life with both hands, although they were actually travelling quite slowly. 'Now a tree that's turned into a lift!'

'Perhaps now isn't the time to tell you that it isn't a real letterbox either.'

'Yes it is, I posted your letter in it yesterday.'

'I know. It was just a note to Imogen. That's how we knew you were about to change. That letterbox can only be seen by Finwips. It's a useful way to communicate with the village.'

'Well, I've heard it all now,' said Alice, shaking her head in disbelief and feeling rather stupid. 'What village?'

There was a gentle thud as the lift stopped. The door slid open and the smell of freshly baked banana bread and bubbling raspberry jam greeted them as their eyes adjusted to the light.

'This one!' said Thomas triumphantly.

Chapter 4

A Village Underground

With trepidation, Alice stepped out into a long, vaulted passageway lit by burning torches. Considering they were underground, the village was astonishing. The walls, floor and ceiling were made of stone, as if an army of people had chiselled away for centuries to create their own secret dwelling. At regular intervals, there were round pillars supporting the structure, with great long drapes in thick, burgundy velvet behind them. On the walls, large bunches of herbs had been hung to dry. As Thomas cajoled her along, she noticed wide, arched wooden doors with brass signs on both sides of the passageway. 'TAILOR & DRESSING ROOMS,' she read. 'LIBRARY.' Then at least a dozen doors labelled 'ACCOMMODATION.'

'What an amazing place to stay!' thought Alice. Then she spotted the most peculiar door. 'TO THE STABLES.' She wondered how on earth a horse would fit in that cramped tree lift. Perhaps a miniature pony could squeeze in ... At the end of the passage the space widened and there were three arched doors, the largest, immediately in front of them, labelled 'DINING HALL.' The other two were 'KITCHEN' and 'PANTRY.' Thomas knocked at the dining hall door.

'Are you ready?' he asked Alice. She nodded.

'Come in,' called two female voices.

Thomas pushed the door, which opened with a sinister creak. 'Step inside,' he said.

Alice was dumbfounded. Standing a few paces in front of her were the most divine creatures she had ever seen. Willowy and elegant, with hair flowing down to the waist and gowns made of a shimmering fabric which Alice doubted could be made on earth. But ... most importantly ... they had wings.

'Are they real?' gasped Alice. She swiftly covered her open mouth with her hand, realising how silly that sounded.

'Real Finwips, yes,' answered the blonde one in the burgundy robe. 'Welcome, Alice. I'm Freya.'

'We meet at last!' said the tall brunette in purple. 'I'm Imogen.' She reached out to shake hands. Alice noticed she had lilac streaks in her hair.

She went through the motions of the formal greeting in a daze. She couldn't take her eyes off their wings, even though she had a pair herself. Freya's were smaller than hers, with rounded edges like those of a Holly Blue butterfly. They moved gently from time to time, reminding Alice of a dog wagging its tail when it's pleased. Imogen's wings behaved in the same way, though hers were much larger, even compared to Alice's. She had to admit, they were stylish – if wings could be stylish – in the shape of a Comma butterfly's wings but with a delicate, lace-like transparency.

'I hope the sight of our wings reassures you,' said Imogen. 'I see yours are yet to retract. May we?' she asked, nodding at Alice's blanket-clad back.

'Oh, yes, of course,' she replied. She let the blanket fall and turned to the side so they could see her wings properly.

'Good grief!' exclaimed Imogen. 'I predicted something impressive, but these are quite remarkable for a Finwip so young. Swallowtail butterfly, I'd say. What do you think, Freya?'

'Most definitely,' agreed Freya. 'They're beautiful.'

While Imogen circled Alice, as if admiring a statue in a museum with an experienced, critical eye, Alice noticed a tear at the bottom of her dress.

'I recognise that material,' she said. 'That happened in my garden, didn't it?'

Imogen looked down and smiled. 'It certainly did. Sorry if I made you nervous when I was checking on you – I was worried. And impatient, if I'm honest. I certainly wasn't expecting to encounter an enormous dog! He jumped up and managed to snap at my robe as I flew off.'

'I'll fix that,' said Freya. 'I shall be making a robe for Alice tomorrow.' As the village tailor, she had been studying Alice's wings as well, planning a robe that would complement them. They referred to them as robes, though they were actually full-length dresses with a long, embroidered velvet cloak. In the back there were slits, specially designed to fit around wing bases. The detail was so intricate, it looked as though human or Finwip hands would struggle with the tiny stitches.

'I do it all myself,' Freya clarified, noticing Alice's approving glances at her needlework. 'Your robe will be a work of art, I promise.'

'I can't wait!' said Alice. 'But when do I wear it? Only when I come here?'

'That's right,' replied Freya. 'We have dressing rooms to get changed on arrival. We try to maintain the traditional dress down here, it's a reminder of our heritage. Plus, who wouldn't want to wear one of these?' she grinned, swishing her cloak around her.

'What colour will mine be?' Alice asked.

'The colours are significant,' explained Freya. 'Yours will be blue, which represents intelligence. Mine is burgundy because I create useful things with my hands. The cooks wear the same colour as me – I suppose we're classed as craftspeople.'

'And Imogen?'

'Purple is for rare or unknown gifts.'

'Is that what Thomas wears, then?'

'Well, no! In his case, we're almost certain his gift will be science-based, so he wears silver-grey.'

'It all sounds very complicated. Do I get to put coloured streaks in my hair too?'

'You won't need to, don't you worry about that. As you get older, they simply appear in your Finwip colour. It won't happen until after you've left school, though, so it's not a problem.'

Alice was sure it would be a problem for her parents, no matter how old she was when her hair turned blue. She could see some pink-ish roots appearing in Freya's hair when she bent down.

'Of course, on a practical level,' Freya continued, 'you need at least one outfit that will accommodate your wings. We all take the opportunity to release them down here. If you don't let them out regularly, they become weak and you will start to feel ill.'

'But how do I get them back in?' asked Alice. 'I need to go back to school.'

'They usually retreat when you are calm,' replied Imogen. 'As a rule, they emerge when we experience strong emotions or fear – like a fight or flight response. Though nowadays, very few of us can fly. If they are being stubborn and don't retreat of their own accord, there is a spray we apply to the base of our wings which works immediately.'

'And you already have that,' piped up Thomas, who had sat down at a table behind them. 'The blue bottle I gave you.'

Alice nodded thoughtfully while Imogen and Freya measured her wings. She looked around the dining room for the first time. It was a circular room of immense proportions, lit by the same burning torches as the passageway. In the centre of the room was a large fire, with an over-sized cooking pot suspended over it from a giant wrought-iron tripod. This was where the raspberry jam smell was coming from. Around the fire was an open space for working (or performing perhaps, Alice imagined) and around this, two huge C-shaped dining tables, each with twenty-four stools. Photographs of past celebrations in the dining room adorned the walls.

At the far end of the room was a sort of cave which enabled you to see part of the kitchen, where Alice could watch people working and identify that aroma of banana bread. A small man in a brown cloak caught sight of her and bowed with an elaborate arm gesture. How strange, she thought, averting her gaze. She could see silver platters piled high with fresh fruit and she cringed as she thought of her last art lesson. Down here, all her worries and embarrassment were slipping away. Shame she couldn't stay. Around the outside of the room were smaller caves or alcoves, each with curved bench seating and a table.

'We don't often eat together,' said Thomas, following her gaze. 'The practicalities of our lives above ground mean that we turn up whenever we can. There's always a warm welcome and plenty of food.'

'Which is what we need now,' decided Imogen. She put down her tape measure and Freya rushed off to her studio with her notes. Sitting down next to Thomas, Imogen signalled to someone in the kitchen.

'Are you in charge here?' asked Alice.

'I suppose I am,' replied Imogen with a smile. 'Though I don't tell people that. It sounds rather pompous! Over the years, Finwips here have come to regard me as their adviser. I help them as much as I can and organise the gatherings down here. Fortunately, I have retired from my job above ground, so I have the time to focus on our community.

Alice was astounded. Retired? Imogen looked so young! Thomas cast a warning glance in her direction.

'It's alright,' Imogen assured him. 'She should know the truth. I'm ninety-two, Alice.'

Alice couldn't prevent her mouth from falling open and she made no attempt to cover it this time.

'My ability is that I no longer age,' Imogen continued. 'At the age of thirty, my ageing process stopped. Hence my role as adviser – years of wisdom, but without the wrinkled brow, you see.'

Alice didn't see at all. 'Does that mean you are going to live forever?' she asked.

'Who knows?' Imogen shrugged her shoulders, making her wings twitch. 'I seem to be the first Finwip with this gift, so only time will tell.'

Alice leaned to the side, as someone reached over them to put a tray on the table.

'Do excuse me, Alice,' said a strangely familiar voice. She turned to see bandana lady from The Coffee Cauldron standing behind her.

'I'm so pleased you're finally here,' she beamed. 'That's a fine pair of wings my love and you've some colour in your cheeks now. Enjoy!' she instructed in her usual manner, waving at the tray of delights and scuttled back to the kitchen.

'Tuck in,' insisted Imogen. Thomas passed over a plate piled with slices of warm banana bread, followed by a large jar of homemade raspberry jam, a bowl of fresh banana and raspberries and a glass of something pink.

'Pomegranate juice,' he said, pushing it in front of her.

Alice didn't respond. What was bandana lady doing down here in the village? Had she been spying on her above ground as well? Her head was spinning in confusion.

'Fay is one of us as well. She has been worried about you for a few weeks, she thought you looked ill,' Imogen explained. She noticed Alice's perplexed expression. 'Fay knew about your symptoms. We can't actually identify a Finwip when we encounter one until a year after their metamorphosis. The obvious trait is that most of us have green eyes, but with experience we somehow sense one another.'

'She doesn't appear to have any wings,' Alice observed, dolloping jam onto her bread with a dessert spoon.

'As odd as this may sound, you don't need to have wings to be a Finwip. Some of us have pointed ears; some of us are rather small.'

'But perfectly formed,' pointed out a bearded face with a grin. A very short man bowed to Alice. He stoked the fire with a poker as tall as himself. He was no more than a metre tall, with pointed ears as well.

'Bandana ... I mean, Fay, has pointed ears?' said Alice, in consternation.

'Obviously,' said Thomas with a mouth full of bread. 'Why do you think she wears that bandana, silly?'

Only then did Alice realise that she had never noticed Fay's ears. The scarf covered the top of them. She rolled her eyes, acknowledging her naivety and carried on eating. As she looked around, she became aware that the torches never changed. That is, considering they were simply burning sticks, neither the wood nor the flame ever changed in appearance. She stared at them intently.

'Finwip technology,' Thomas informed her. 'Just like the main fire. Burning without fuel.'

Alice sighed. She pushed her plate away and plucked up the courage to ask Imogen the question that had been frazzling her brain since her wings appeared.

'Imogen ... please can you explain to me what we are, exactly? I mean, I know we're winged people, but why are we like this? And why us?' Her voice began to waver with emotion. 'My life has been turned upside down and I don't even understand why.'

Imogen turned to face her and held her hands tightly. 'Well, in basic terms ... you've heard of woodland folk in story books when you were younger?'

Alice nodded.

'Those tales contain an element of truth. Nowadays we do not refer to ourselves as woodland folk or fairies. Those names are considered very patronising. We are descendants from that society but we have evolved greatly to adapt to modern life. Our ancestors were persecuted by normal humans until they became a race in hiding.'

'We're still hiding from humans though, aren't we?'

'To a degree, yes. But now we can all have a normal life above ground, which they didn't have. I prefer to think that Finwips have the privilege of an additional secret life that opens up more opportunities.'

'Opportunities for people at school to tease me.'

'It won't last,' asserted Imogen. 'We're a peaceful, intelligent race and your classmates will soon tire of it when they realise that your achievements will continue regardless of their behaviour. That's the trouble with humans, so many of them still mock intelligence instead of respecting it.'

Alice wrinkled up her nose, unconvinced. 'What about the fruit cravings? Will they stop?'

'They won't stop, but they certainly won't be as strong now that your wings have developed. You must always carry fruit with you. We'll give you some recipes as well, which will satisfy your requirement for longer. Our need for the vitamins from fruit and vegetables is far greater than that of humans because our bodies are more complicated. We all grow our own vegetables above ground and bring any spare down here – I know you do that already, which is good. You might notice that you become more healthy than your classmates as you get older. Then who will have the last laugh? No colds and fewer spots!'

Alice managed a smile. Thomas nodded in agreement. 'It's true,' he said. 'Look how gorgeous I am!'

Imogen laughed as Alice pulled a face in disgust.

'I think that's enough information for today,' she said. 'You're clearly still on edge because those wings haven't retracted yet. I'll fetch a spray.'

She went to a large cupboard and came back with a blue bottle identical to the one that Thomas had given her. 'Shall I do the honours?' she asked.

'Yes, please,' replied Alice eagerly.

She felt a mist of that familiar cold liquid on her back and within seconds her enormous wings folded themselves up and somehow disappeared beneath her skin. Alice shuddered. It didn't hurt, but felt indescribably odd. She reached round to her back but could feel nothing out of the ordinary. What a huge relief.

'Take this and always keep it with you,' insisted Imogen, handing her the bottle. A short, rotund Finwip with tiny wings and a burgundy robe scuttled over from the kitchen with a folder of recipes. With a brief curtsey she presented it to Alice and as she looked up, Alice recognised her from the canteen at school. The Finwip dinner lady grinned.

'I can recommend the banana and sultana crumble,' she said, before dashing back to the kitchen.

Today couldn't get any more bizarre. Alice put her cardigan back the right way round and Imogen lent her a coat.

'We shall see you again on Saturday,' she informed her. 'As an exception, since you are so young, you can bring your friend - Sarah, isn't it? Thomas and Fay speak highly of her, so it would seem she can be trusted. You will be glad of someone for support when Thomas is back at university. It's unfortunate that such responsibility has fallen on one so young.'

'What responsibility?' asked Alice anxiously. She cast an interrogating look at Thomas, but he shrugged his shoulders, equally puzzled.

'No need to worry,' said Imogen, 'We'll talk about it on Saturday with Sarah. But in the meantime, could you do just one thing for us, Alice?'

'What's that?'

'Try and be friendly towards Lucinda Rowbottom.'

'You must be joking!' exclaimed Alice. 'Really?' she raised an eyebrow.

'I'm afraid so.'

'But she hates me! She's always such a ...'

'Don't let that worry you,' Imogen interrupted. 'Her father's a different matter, though. He's a very cruel man, evil to the core. It will all become clear soon, but that would be extremely helpful if you can manage it.'

'I'll try,' said Alice, pulling a face.

Imogen shook her hand. 'Goodbye for now. It's an honour to have you with us.'

Alice just smiled, bewildered by it all. She walked to the lift with Thomas, in silence. Once inside, Thomas couldn't bite his tongue.

'Well, you must be something special.'

'I don't like you when you're sarcastic.'

'I'm not being sarcastic! I just wish I knew what all the fuss is about!'

'Me too.'

Silence. When the lift stopped at Albany Road, Thomas asked her to press an amber button. Alice saw a vertical row of red, amber and green lights. She did as she was told. Suddenly they could see the street outside. Alice reached out, but the tree-trunk door was still there, just clear, like glass. She shrank back from it as a young woman walked past with a pushchair.

'It's OK, she can't see us,' Thomas reassured her. 'This is similar to one-way glass – it's a safety feature so that we can check no one is around when we emerge from the tree.'

A jogger ran past and Thomas pressed his nose against the door. After a good look in each direction, he instructed,

'All clear, press green.'

The door slid open and Alice darted out from behind him. She had never felt so grateful to be standing on the pavement she walked down most days. Even the chill in the air felt invigorating as it seemed to confirm the reality of her former life. She looked behind her at the perfectly normal, if rather large oak tree. No trace of a door. She shook her head slowly, then checked her watch. Just after 2pm. Good, they would be home well before their parents.

'Relax,' said Thomas. 'Back to school and normality tomorrow.'

For once, Alice didn't object.

Chapter 5

The Act of Being Normal

As she stood in front of the mirror on Thursday morning, Alice felt numb. Looking at her reflection, it was as if nothing had happened during the last few days. Same hair, same uniform with holey tights. Today she was wearing a T-shirt under her shirt, in preparation for getting changed for P.E. – she had to conceal that wing base mark. Turning her back to the mirror, she craned her neck as if she still half expected to see some sort of evidence through her clothes.

She hadn't spoken to Sarah since her metamorphosis on Tuesday and was apprehensive about seeing her again. What should she say? Would Sarah have kept it to herself or let it slip to one of her sisters? If it had been the other way round, Alice very much doubted that she could keep such a massive secret.

As it happened, Sarah didn't mention it initially. She did ask how Alice was feeling after her 'illness', as she called it, but so did Sebastian, surprisingly. There was no sarcastic comment when she approached the classroom door and he even noticed that she didn't look as tired.

'Well spotted,' she thought. 'Not as dumb as he looks, it would seem.' Eventually, she asked Sarah if she had told anyone.

'As if!' she exclaimed. 'Who'd believe me? Good to see you're back to normal, though. Whatever normal is, these days.'

'Thanks,' said Alice quietly.

'Listen,' Sarah continued. 'When you've got two sisters, you know how to keep secrets.'

Of course. Alice hadn't thought of that. For now, her focus was on keeping her head down and muddling through until

Saturday, when she hoped that Imogen would explain her role in Finwip society. Or, as far as Alice was concerned at the moment, her purpose in life. She could see how melodramatic that seemed for a thirteen year old.

English passed without incident. This time, Sarah made sure she had read her allocated chapters and Alice wasn't picked on to summarise any today. French did unnerve her, though – she even surprised herself with her fluency and accent. She barely recognised her own voice. But … when Lucinda turned around to pull a face, Alice was ready. She beat her to it, grinning like an idiot and taking a small bow in her seat, silently mouthing the words 'thank you.'

Lucinda wasn't sure how to react. She smiled briefly and turned around to face the front. Seconds later, she turned back and smiled again.

'Ha! It's working!' thought Alice smugly. Although her stomach was churning as she remembered what Imogen had said about Mr Rowbottom. She didn't feel so smug when she noticed the disapproving look that Sarah was giving her, who had no idea why Alice should want to humour anyone from the coven. Alice planned to explain everything later, including Sarah's impending visit to the village. She spent her lunch break doing the geography homework that she had missed the day before, with Sarah's help. Not that she needed help these days, but when her friend began to recount what they had covered in the lesson, she didn't have the heart to interrupt.

After a horrible hockey lesson shivering in the cold and rain, Alice knew for sure that sport was not part of her gifted ability. She certainly wasn't immune to being bashed on the ankles. As they walked back to school from the playing field, Alice took the opportunity to bring Sarah up to date with yesterday's developments. Amazingly, she took it all in calmly and didn't seem at all surprised about Fay from The Coffee Cauldron. However, when the part came about her invitation to the village, she couldn't contain her excitement.

'Oh … my … life! That's going to be brilliant! I can't wait!' she squealed.

'Shhh,' warned Alice, looking over her shoulder nervously. 'They're all quite normal, really.'

'By your standards,' Sarah pointed out.

*

That evening, Thomas had arranged to take Alice to see Grandad Parker. And Grandma, of course. The visit was primarily to introduce Alice to the family Finwip history, though Alice was hoping to interrogate him further about that mysterious kidnapping situation. Thomas was using the excuse that he had bought Grandad some of his favourite fudge from the shop in Oxford.

During dinner, her mother asked if she had caught up after missing a day of school yesterday.

'Oh yes, I didn't miss that much. I've done the homework already.'

'Good. We don't want you to slip now that you're doing so well,' said her mother, satisfied.

'You've done well for someone who had a bad stomach yesterday!' commented her father, nodding at her empty plate.

'Er … well, I *was* hungry. We've been playing hockey this afternoon. And I feel much better today,' Alice replied, worried that he was suspicious.

'Must have been that rotten twenty-four hour bug that's going round at the moment,' he said.

'Probably,' Thomas joined in. 'I know a lot of people who've had what Alice had yesterday.'

Clever, conceded Alice in silent admiration. She breathed a sigh of relief. Thankfully her mother changed the subject.

'What are you going to do with yourself in the holidays?' she asked. 'You break up in a few days!'

'Nothing much,' said Alice. Although she intended to spend time getting to know the village and its inhabitants.

Her father asked if any Christmas parties were coming up. Thomas had already been to lavish Christmas parties in Oxford before term ended. Their term ended at the beginning of December, over a fortnight before Alice finished school. Some people have all the luck.

'I haven't been invited to any yet,' Alice confessed, feeling rather ashamed. She described enviously the previous Christmas parties she had heard about that the Rowbottoms had thrown. They lived in an enormous house, like a stately home, with acres of land and their own stables. Even a live-in maid, so Katy Smackwell had once told everyone. Apparently, there had been a Father Christmas at last year's party with real reindeer outside and wonderful presents for everyone. Katy received a silver fountain pen engraved with her name. Olivia got a silver bracelet with her initial and a blue stone, Alice had seen it. On that occasion, blue couldn't have been chosen to represent intelligence …

'I don't trust that man,' said her father. 'I was only there last week. Someone reported a man lying outside his gates and we were sent out to him. I won't go into detail, but he was in a bad way.'

'What happened there, then?' asked Thomas.

'Well, it seemed obvious to us, but Brian Rowbottom insisted he'd never seen the man before. Conveniently, the CCTV camera on the gates wasn't working.'

Alice felt queasy. She was glad she'd finished her vegetable risotto …

After dinner, she went upstairs to get ready while Thomas helped clear the table. She felt strangely anxious. It was only her grandad they were visiting, but she saw him in a different light now. Would he expect her to behave differently now she was a Finwip? More to the point, why hadn't he and Thomas warned her earlier what was happening? All those weeks of feeling ill and confused. Anger began to well up as she thought about it – she slammed her hairbrush down on the desk and kicked the wardrobe door to close it.

There she was again! That blonde girl in the mirror who looked perfectly normal, but was gradually realising she was anything but.

Chapter 6

Revelations

Thomas borrowed his mother's Mini to drive them to Stonethorpe village, which was about four miles away. He always felt silly driving a tiny blue car with the Union Jack painted on the roof, but Alice loved it. Grandma and Grandad Parker lived in a thatched bungalow in what tourists might describe as a picturesque, traditional English village. Theirs was one of a cluster of black and white cottages arranged around the village green, with a red telephone box and a grocery shop. Alice remembered buying sweets there when she was small and she would have now, if it had been open. The green certainly wasn't green tonight. It was covered in snow, glistening beneath the white lights of the magnificent Christmas tree in the centre. Alice looked forward to seeing it every year – so did Thomas, not that he would admit it.

Grandad was a professional photographer. Although he had reached retirement age long ago, he still worked because photography was his passion. Grandma was from Germany originally, but had moved to England in her teens and trained to become a midwife. She, however, had retired and spent much of her time baking fantastic cakes. Alice was hoping for a masterpiece this evening.

On arrival, there were hugs all round. Her grandparents congratulated her, as if she had achieved something wonderful, rather than being an unwitting participant in events that were making life rather awkward. Alice hadn't even been sure that Grandma would know about Finwips, but clearly Grandad kept nothing from her, which was a good thing.

It looked promising for a cake: Grandma wiped some flour off her rosy cheeks and rubbed her hands briskly on her apron. As she smoothed down her thick, mousey hair, she noticed

Alice's uneasy body language. She seemed restless, twiddling the buttons on her coat.

'Your grandad and I met when we were just eighteen, you know. His wings didn't present themselves until two years later and we were married by then. I always knew he was an odd one, but I wasn't expecting that, I can tell you!' she joked.

Alice smiled.

'She's not complaining, she loves the Finwips and all the social gatherings in the village,' said Grandad. 'They love her too, for all the cakes she provides!'

They went through to the lounge, where they sat down around the dinner table. It was old-fashioned and cosy, with an open fire, dark wooden furniture and tapestry seat covers. You could scarcely see any wallpaper for all the framed photographs that Grandad had taken over the years. It reminded Alice of cave paintings, since you could look around and follow the history of their life. Dotted here and there were Grandma's reminders of Germany: a brightly-coloured Bierkrug with a metal lid, a matchbox-sized Trabant toy car and an extensive collection of books that Alice couldn't read. Mind you, perhaps she could if she tried now. Would she be fluent in German although she hadn't started to learn it yet?

Laid out on the table were photo albums, scrap-books and an old biscuit_tin full of black and white photographs. Grandad rummaged in the tin until he found a small photo which he passed to Alice. 'That was taken the day after my metamorphosis,' he explained. 'Of course, I wouldn't have taken any photos if I hadn't been able to develop them myself. I couldn't risk taking them to a shop.'

Thomas had seen them all before. He took the fudge from his coat pocket and handed it to his grandad.

'Ah, that's the stuff! Rum and raisin. Good lad, thank you.' He started on it straight away. 'I'm not sharing, you understand,' he mumbled with his mouth full.

'They won't be needing fudge,' said Grandma promptly. 'I made their favourite, Pflaumenkuchen.' She went out to the kitchen.

'Yum!' said Alice with a grin, as she began to analyse the photograph. There was her grandad in a dimly-lit room with the curtains drawn. It had been taken sideways-on to show the size and detail of his wings. He described them as Serotine bat wings, but they had the usual transparent characteristics of Finwip wings. Grandad certainly looked peculiar with wings, not to mention the short trousers and hideous patterned shirt. But more importantly, it was a comforting insight for Alice.

'So who helped you when you changed?' she asked him.

'My boss, when I was an apprentice photographer. As a Finwip himself, he saw the signs, which is why he took me on.'

'That was lucky,' said Alice, intrigued.

'It certainly was,' agreed Grandma, as she brought the colossal Pflaumenkuchen and a bottle of apple juice to the table. 'I don't know what we'd have done otherwise.'

'It's not really down to luck,' Grandad continued. 'No one is left alone for their metamorphosis. There's always a Finwip watching over a newcomer. All Finwip communities make sure of that. That's why you'll find a lot of them working in schools and colleges on the look-out for developments.'

'And cafes, it would seem,' added Thomas.

'What, all over the country?' asked Alice, wide-eyed.

Grandad nodded in a matter-of-fact manner while Thomas tried to keep a straight face.

'All over the world, Alice,' Grandad clarified. 'Though we're not keen on very hot climates, they make our wings dry and uncomfortable.'

'I just can't believe it,' declared Alice, helping herself to a slice of cake. 'I can't believe that there must be thousands of us. Which means there must be hundreds of Finwip groups underground all over the world. Anywhere you go you could be walking on top of a village! Mmm, this cake is delicious – I love plums.'

'You'll find that holidays are much more fun if you find the local Finwip village,' revealed Grandma. 'Especially in Germany, my, the stories we could tell you!'

'Could, but won't yet!' interrupted Grandad.

'What's your special gift, then?' asked Alice, gulping down her apple juice.

'Just the photography, as far as I know. I'm classed as an artist anyway, I wear a gold cloak. I took most of the photographs in the Finwip dining hall, you might have seen them.'

Alice nodded.

'So your gift is super-intelligence?'

'I think so,' replied Alice modestly.

'Lucky you,' said Grandad. 'That's the best gift as far as I'm concerned. Worth having and useful on so many levels. It will earn you respect as well.'

'Hmm,' grunted Alice. 'It hasn't yet. Anyway, why didn't you tell me what was going on? I've been living a nightmare for weeks, muddling through on my own and no one said anything.'

'Well, you may have *felt* alone, but you weren't, I can assure you. As well as Thomas and myself, who recognised your symptoms, there have been several Finwips watching over you from a distance. We have to be one hundred percent sure, which means waiting until the final transformation. Our community must be protected, we can't risk anyone finding out.'

Alice looked less than impressed. 'I can't believe you never told Dad what you are.'

A look of guilt swept over Grandad's face. 'I had my reasons. In some ways, Alice, your dad was a lot like you when he was at school. He felt he didn't fit in, and took a lot of stick from the other kids. Largely because of me.'

Alice frowned.

'He went to a good school; a grammar school, where most of the dads wore a suit and drove a flash car. Then there was me, the photographer with long hair, foppish clothes and an old heap of a vehicle. I was an embarrassment to Mike. In the end, he preferred to walk home. All he wanted was to be like the other kids. Of course, it didn't help matters that he was a chubby lad. He's always liked his food!'

'So you didn't want to make him feel any worse,' Alice realised.

'Exactly. I never had the heart to tell him, even when he grew up. He's so proud of his family. I'm not sure how he'd react if he knew that you and Thomas were ... different.'

'I can understand that,' said Alice quietly.

'Listen,' said Thomas. 'I don't want this to sound like sibling rivalry, but have you any idea why Alice is so important? To the Finwip community, I mean.'

'You haven't been told yet?'

'No,' Alice and Thomas replied simultaneously.

Grandma tutted in disapproval and cast a meaningful glance at her husband.

'Oh, OK. For what it's worth, I believe it's about Theo,' he admitted.

Thomas frowned, failing to see the significance.

'Who's Theo?' asked Alice.

'He's one of the oldest and wisest members of our village,' said Thomas. 'He can predict numerical results. But he vanished a few weeks ago.'

'You mean he was kidnapped,' said Alice.

'WHAT?' Thomas looked shocked.

Grandad nodded. 'I'm afraid he didn't just vanish. We're almost certain he was kidnapped by you-know-who, so that they can exploit his ability.'

Thomas was appalled. 'You mean the Sinwips?'

'Who else? Do you think it's pure coincidence that there have been three big lottery wins in Warwickshire in the last six weeks? I suppose they think it's less obvious, leaving a fortnight's gap in between.'

'Who's they?' asked Alice.

'Brian Rowbottom and his brother mainly – though he pockets the lion's share of the money. If you don't believe me, look at this.'

He fetched the local Courier newspaper from his armchair and laid it on the table in front of them. Tonight's headline read, 'Local businessman buys Aylesford Castle.'

'How do you think he got the money for that? You're talking an eight figure sum.'

'I heard that on the news,' said Alice. 'That's Lucinda's dad,' she said, pointing at the self-satisfied man in the photograph.

'Correct. Brian is bound to be at the bottom of this.'

Thomas smirked. 'Witty.'

Alice was lost now.

'I still don't … I mean, what are Sinwips?' she asked.

'I'm ashamed to say that they're Finwips but with an evil streak,' replied Grandad. 'They're not a different breed, they just have no morals. Hence the name they've acquired from us. They're all tainted, that's why we have separate communities. We just don't get on. You see, Alice, in true Finwip society it's forbidden to use our gift for personal gain, that is, in a deceitful way. If you can earn a living above ground from photography or painting or, for example, if you became a teacher, that's fine. But we mustn't exploit it for the wrong reasons.'

'So you're saying Lucinda's dad, Brian Rowbottom, is a Sinwip?'

'Their leader, I'm afraid.'

'He's kidnapped Theo to make money out of him?'

'Exactly. So far he's predicted three sets of winning lottery numbers. And did you hear about the bank robbery at the weekend? The thieves knew the combination of the safe.'

'That was Brian as well?' gasped Alice.

'The name 'Brian' doesn't quite have the ring of a supervillain, does it?' joked Thomas.

'He's been called worse, I can assure you,' said Grandad, though he wasn't laughing. He reached for one of the scrapbooks. 'I'm not usually wrong on these things,' he maintained. 'Look at these. I took them last week outside his house.'

The first photograph he pointed to showed Brian Rowbottom driving a brand new black Bentley, waiting for his electric gates to open. The second photograph, taken with a zoom lens, was of a new Porsche with a personal number plate for his wife. It was parked in one of their five garages.

'Himmelswillen! John, you'll be arrested for spying one of these days!' declared Grandma, horrified at what she saw.

'I'm always careful,' he replied indignantly. 'How do you think the Rowbottoms can suddenly afford all this? Only a few months ago their property business was on the verge of collapse.'

Alice rested her elbows on the table and dragged her fingers through her hair in frustration. 'Will someone please tell me what all this has got to do with me?' she wailed.

Grandma put her arm around Alice's shoulders. 'I think you're their way in, my love,' she said softly.

'What?' said Alice, none the wiser for her grandma's insight.

'Fate has thrown us a lifeline called Alice Parker!' explained Grandad.

'You said the person who could help Theo didn't exist!' said Alice defiantly.

'I should have added *yet*. Not only do you know Rowbottom's daughter, but no one in his community knows that you're one of us yet. There's a twelve month maturing process following the metamorphosis before you can be sniffed out by another Finwip. Even then, those without wings remain difficult to detect.'

'I don't follow,' admitted Alice.

'Before your metamorphosis, we could guess what you were from your symptoms – sugar cravings, back ache, the onset of your ability. Mature Finwips can recognise each other just by ... well ... being in close proximity. We don't know how, exactly. You won't be sniffed out for a year.'

'Sniffed out? Well that's just marvellous,' snapped Alice. 'As if it's not enough to turn into a fairy after school on Tuesday, it now sounds like I'm going to be sent on a mission to rescue some weird old bloke!'

'WE'RE NOT FAIRIES!' shouted Thomas and his grandad defiantly.

'So you say.'

'They are,' mouthed Grandma silently to Alice, as she walked out to the kitchen.

'And Theo isn't weird,' muttered Grandad.

Alice could feel her eyes starting to well up with tears but she fought them back. 'Why me? There must be someone else who can do it. This is a mistake.'

Grandad shook his head. 'It has to be someone who can get an invitation to the Rowbottom's Christmas ball at the castle – we think that's where Theo is being held. It's heavily guarded by day and night, with dogs patrolling after dark. According to our insider, Daniel, the only time it won't be guarded is the night of the ball. He's a Finwip without wings, who for some reason can't be detected at all, but as a daytime employee, he can't be at the party. Plus, he's terrified of losing his job.'

'So why can't one of you adults sneak in?' demanded Alice.

'The risk is too great,' replied Grandad. 'If Brian identifies a Finwip on his property, they're in trouble. Unless they're paying to visit the castle during the day – we've tested that already. He doesn't refuse our money.'

Alice didn't like the sound of this at all.

'Don't upset yourself, it's all a bit overwhelming, I understand that,' said Grandad calmly. 'But you haven't just got us to support you, you've got a whole community of Finwips. The difference is that you're very young. And fortunately, perfectly placed to help us out.'

'But I just want to be normal,' she whined, with her head in her hands.

'You are normal. A perfectly normal Finwip.'

*

In the car on the way home, Alice sat with her arms folded and a scowl on her face. Thomas could sense how bad it was, even in the dark.

'Oh, Alice, cheer up will you? It's great being a Finwip and I thought you liked the village?'

'I do. But I don't need any more hassle. I get enough of that at school.'

'School should be a breeze now, with your ability.'

'Bah! Easy for you to say! You don't get teased for being brainy in Oxford, do you? You're all brainy, that's why you're there.'

'They're only jealous, Alice. They may be popular now, trying to be cool by not making an effort, but they'll regret it later. You'll have a rewarding job while they're cleaning toilets, or sweeping the floor at a hairdresser's.'

'I can't see Lucinda cleaning a toilet!'

'Well, next time she and her mates are giving you grief, just imagine her doing that and smile sweetly. You've got to pretend to be nice, anyway.'

'I don't do nice.'

'Really? And there I was thinking what exquisite company you've been this evening.'

'Just shut up and drive,' snapped Alice, unable to hide the smile emerging from her annoyance.

'Touché.'

Chapter 7

A Close Shave

Friday morning brought more top marks at school. Alice knew today would be difficult, having to face Lucinda after what she had discovered last night – she could have done without an A+ for her science project. She had forgotten all about it, having handed it in a fortnight ago. The results weren't read out, but Lawrence turned round from the bench in front and saw the grade on Alice's folder. Within seconds, everyone knew her result. The usual noises of discontent could be heard. Katy Smackwell excelled herself, flopping down on the workbench and pretending to put her mouth over a gas tap. The coven was in hysterics. Alice wished she had the power to turn on that gas tap with her mind. Telekinesis would have been a much better gift than intelligence, she thought.

As Lucinda turned around to pull a predictable face, Alice remembered what Thomas had said about her cleaning toilets. She fabricated the biggest smile she could manage. In fact, the more she thought about Lucinda using a toilet brush, the more she wanted to laugh out loud. The expression of concentration on her face, as she struggled to maintain that smile without splitting her sides, made Alice look both insane and menacing. Clearly alarmed by this, Lucinda turned back to face the front.

Sarah was snorting with mirth. She actually thought Alice had mastered that expression purposely to confuse Lucinda. Unfortunately, that wasn't the case, but Alice wasn't going to let on. Hey, it had worked and she hadn't even opened her mouth.

Sadly, Alice's self-satisfaction was to be short-lived. At break-time, she and Sarah went to the school hall for the charity cake sale. Sarah had brought in a Victoria sponge this morning. In light of recent events, Alice had forgotten to bring anything. Still, at least she could buy plenty, as each class had its own stall. Sebastian was organising theirs with Lydia, one of the quieter girls in their class.

The coven was already at the Year 8 stall choosing their cakes. 'Fairy cake, Alice?' asked Lucinda. Alice started to go red. Did she know something? Or was she just trying to be nice?

'More like a goblin cake, judging by that daft face earlier,' said Katy. The coven giggled.

'At least that face wasn't permanent,' replied Alice, looking at Katy in pity.

Lydia chortled.

'What's funny?' demanded Lucinda, irritated by Alice's wit. 'Have you only just seen your new haircut in the mirror?'

Lydia's face fell. Alice and Sarah were mortified – no one was nasty to Lydia, she was too nice.

Alice looked down at the floor and spotted Lucinda's new shoes. They were hideous, shiny black dolly shoes with a bow on the front.

'It seems money can't buy taste,' she remarked, nudging Sarah. Everyone laughed except the coven, though Olivia couldn't help smiling briefly. Alice regretted it as soon as she had said it. Imogen wouldn't be pleased at all.

Lucinda was furious and couldn't think of a comeback. Red-faced, she turned to look at the cakes on the table. 'Which one did you make?' she asked Sarah.

'That one,' she replied proudly, pointing at the impressive sponge, oozing with jam and cream.

Lucinda looked at it closely. 'There's something missing,' she said, and spat out her chewing gum on top of it. Sarah shrieked. Sebastian pushed Lucinda away in disgust.

'You're sick,' he concluded, shaking his head. 'Just like …'

He was interrupted by what sounded like a war cry from Alice. Full of rage, she lunged towards Lucinda but Sarah just managed to pull her back by her blazer.

'Don't,' she pleaded. 'It's not worth getting into trouble.'

But it was too late for that. Alice felt a familiar burning sensation across her upper back. Horrified, she broke free from Sarah and raced out of the hall and down the corridor towards the toilets, pulling her rucksack off her back as she went.

She darted into a cubicle, slammed the door and took off her blazer. She knew what was coming and pressed her clammy hands and forehead against the cool door. Sure enough, as she stood hunched over and sweating, those formidable wings tore though her shirt once again. She heard rapid footsteps – Sarah had followed her.

'Alice, are you alright?' she called anxiously. She banged on the door of the cubicle. 'That is you isn't it? There's no one else in here.'

'Don't let anyone in!' ordered Alice. 'Especially not Lucinda!' Sarah could hear the panic in her voice.

'Why, are you ill?'

'Not exactly,' she whispered. 'Look up.'

Sarah saw the tips of two glorious wings quivering above the cubicle.

'Oh, no,' she sighed in dismay, darting to the door. She looked out into the corridor to make sure no one was coming. Sebastian was right outside and made her jump.

'Is everything OK in there?' he asked. 'Lydia sent me to find out.'

'Er, no. Stand outside this door and don't let anyone in. Alice isn't well.'

Sebastian nodded, looking worried.

Sarah dashed back in. 'What can I do Alice?' she asked. Alice kicked her rucksack under the door.

'There's a blue glass bottle in the front pocket – could you pass it to me please? I've no room to move around.'

She found it straight away.

'Can you pass it over the top? I can't even bend down I'm so cramped in here.'

Sarah was rather short and couldn't reach over the door, so she went into the next cubicle and stood on the toilet. She looked down at her friend over the partition wall. 'Oh, dear,' she said calmly. At least she was prepared this time.

'Can you do me a favour and spray my back at the base of the wings please,' asked Alice.

Sarah knew the spray wasn't close enough to reach, so she climbed up onto the cistern and leaned over. One foot slipped, pushing off the ceramic cover, which fell to the ground with an almighty crash. Sarah was fine, perched on the partition, but the door to the corridor flew open.

Sebastian stuck his head round.

'What was that? Is everything alright?'

He looked up and saw a guilty-looking Sarah sitting on the partition wall. A bemused expression came over his face and he scurried out, closing the door behind him.

Alice had tried to crouch down to hide the top of her wings.

'It's OK, he's gone,' Sarah confirmed. She sprayed her friend's back where her shirt had ripped open and was amazed as she watched the huge, damp, but strangely beautiful butterfly wings fold themselves neatly back under Alice's skin.

Alice breathed a sigh of relief. 'Thanks,' she sighed, sounding exhausted.

'Any time,' said Sarah as she jumped down. 'But you've got to learn to control your temper. Lucinda deserved whatever you were going to do – I'd love to see her get a good slap! But you need to remember these wings.'

'I know,' said Alice quietly. 'You're right. But it makes me mad when she's so nasty! She shouldn't get away with it.' Nor should her father – though she thought it best not to tell

Sarah about Brian Rowbottom until tomorrow. Even she might lose her cool when she heard about the kidnapping.

'Do you want to swap shirts?' asked Sarah. 'Your mum will be suspicious if you lose another one this week. I can tell mine I caught my back on something.'

'Oh, yes please,' replied Alice gratefully. 'That *would* save some explaining, thanks.'

Eventually, they both emerged from the toilets and Alice opened the door to thank Sebastian for keeping watch.

'Everything alright now?' he asked. Alice nodded, though wondering how she would get through the rest of the day. Sebastian smiled and rushed off.

'Sorry about that Sarah. Are you still OK for tomorrow, I haven't put you off coming to the village, have I?' asked Alice.

'Of course you haven't. Nothing will surprise me any more where you're concerned. I think I'm lucky, there can't be many people who have a friend with wings.'

'Don't you believe it,' said Alice. 'Just wait and see.'

Chapter 8

Another Transformation

Alice felt quite peeved that Sarah took to the tree lift immediately. Thomas was with them – it had been useful to tell their parents that he would walk into town with them. As a rule, he slept for most of the day on Saturdays, but used the excuse of Christmas shopping to leave the house with the girls this morning. A far cry from Alice's initial mistrust of the lift, when she held on until her knuckles were white, Sarah was thoroughly enjoying herself, as if on a ride at the fair.

'I can hardly believe this!' she declared, smiling, her eyes darting everywhere as they travelled below ground.

'Stop it,' said Alice, annoyed. 'You look an idiot, grinning like that. You're supposed to act like a mature, responsible friend when we get there.'

'Alright, alright. I'm new to this. You have to admit though, it is brilliant, a lift inside a tree. Give me that.'

'Oh, I suppose so,' replied Alice, wishing she could be as laid-back as her friend. Perhaps Imogen and Fay were right to think that Sarah was a positive influence. She certainly had been a good friend lately, there was no denying that.

At first Sarah hadn't believed Alice when she told her about Theo being kidnapped by Lucinda's father.

'NO WAY!' she screeched. 'No wonder you went for her yesterday! I'll never be able to look at her in the same way again.'

They stepped out into the corridor and Alice sent the lift back up for her brother, who was waiting. There wasn't room for three people in there.

Sarah looked around, studying everything in detail. 'Incredible,' she declared. 'All this down here and we've been walking over it every day without knowing.'

'I know what you mean,' agreed Alice, beginning to feel quite proud to be part of it.

The lift arrived and Thomas stepped out.

'Greetings, earthlings!' he said in his very best alien voice, waving his arms in a welcoming gesture. 'Let me take you to our leader!' Alice rolled her eyes and shook her head at his daft behaviour. He pushed in front of them and led them to the door of the library.

'I'll leave you to it,' he said. 'You don't need me this morning. I'm going to let my wings out and see what's to eat. Good luck.'

'Wait! How do you make your wings come out?' asked Alice. 'When you want them to, I mean.'

'Rather than in the loo at school?' joked Thomas. 'Imogen will show you a quick and easy way for now. The other method takes a while to master.' He disappeared into the changing rooms.

Alice took a deep breath and knocked on the library door. Imogen called them in. She stood up to greet them and held out her hand to Sarah.

'Very glad to meet you,' she said. 'I've heard a lot about you.'

Sarah shook hands. She couldn't take her eyes off Imogen's exquisite robes and fantastic lilac-streaked hair.

'Why haven't you got your wings out today, Imogen?' asked Alice, disappointed that her friend couldn't see them.

'We shall be going outside shortly,' she explained. 'We can let our wings out afterwards.'

They sat down opposite Imogen on a large, brown leather sofa. This room was new to Alice too and they both looked around in awe. The ceiling had wooden beams, possibly just for decoration, and the wooden floor was adorned with three vast patterned rugs. Around each rug were three sofas and four small tables, upon which tall glass lanterns with real flames were positioned to light the room. Everything was arranged symmetrically, which Alice liked. On the two longer sides were bookcases from floor to ceiling and at the end of the room where they were sitting, a wonderful open fire. Botanical drawings adorned the walls and were also embroidered on the cushions.

'As you have gathered, Alice, you have a very important role here,' began Imogen.

'Is this to do with finding Theo?' Alice interrupted. She didn't want Imogen to beat around the bush.

'Yes … I suppose your grandad guessed? John's very sharp, he doesn't miss a trick!'

Alice nodded.

'In Finwip communities we look after each other. The safety of every one of us has a direct impact on all of us. For example, if the police were involved, questions would be asked and secrets discovered.'

'Surely that's a good thing?' asked Sarah, puzzled.

'Not if you're a Finwip. They would want to know why he was kidnapped, why he has a special ability and then tests may be carried out. They might discover his wings and then our communities. Our peaceful Finwip society would be finished, we would be treated as mutants.'

Alice was stunned, that hadn't crossed her mind. 'I still don't see why you can't ask someone else, who's not a Finwip,' she protested.

Imogen frowned. 'If an outsider were caught trespassing, they would be 'dealt with', shall we say, by Brian's heavies. If that person went to hospital and the police asked questions, would they hold their tongue? No, because they've nothing to lose. They would tell them we sent them and the secret would be out. The only alternatives are your grandma, who couldn't get an invitation, and Daniel, who won't risk his job at the castle. We also considered another member of Theo's family, but his daughter won't allow it. You can understand her fear.'

Alice nodded. 'What if *I* get caught?' she asked, horrified. 'Will I be 'dealt with' in the same way?'

'I think even Brian would draw the line there,' replied Imogen.

'And if Theo isn't rescued?'

'Brian is making too much money too quickly – greed is clouding his judgement. People have noticed how many businesses and properties he has bought recently. They are already asking questions.'

'What do I have to do?' Alice asked miserably.

'Well, the first step, as I said before, is to become friends with Lucinda Rowbottom.'

Alice's face fell. 'That's not going well,' she admitted.

'I'd say that's an understatement,' added Sarah.

'Well, one way or another, you need to be invited to the Rowbottoms' Christmas party at the castle. You haven't got long – it's taking place on Saturday evening and you finish school on Wednesday. That gives you three days to work on her.'

'Oh, blimey ... I just don't see how. She's rich, fashionable, horsey ... I don't even know how to ride!'

'That won't be an issue,' Imogen assured her. 'I think we've got something that Lucinda won't be able to resist.' She stood up and fetched a camera from the drawer of a very grand, ornate wooden dresser at the far end of the room. 'Follow me,' she said with a smile.

She led them to the stables, which they were dismayed to find empty, apart from a stable hand who looked suspiciously like a pixie.

'The animals only come down here at night, for safety,' he explained when he saw their disillusioned faces.

Oddly, there was natural light in here coming through small shafts in the ceiling. Imogen opened some double doors which Alice had assumed housed a store cupboard. She stepped inside a pleasantly spacious lift and beckoned them in. It was big enough for a horse.

'I much prefer this to the tree lift,' said Alice in approval. The exit was not as pleasing, however. They stepped out into a dingy timber stable building in the corner of a field and could see the horses outside wearing their winter blankets. Imogen went to the door then turned to the girls.

'Please stay calm. These creatures are very sensitive to emotions and don't like any upset.' She cupped her hands around her mouth and gave an unusual, low-pitched whistle. One of the horses, wearing a fancy headdress with a plume, trotted over obligingly. The other two looked over, but went back to grazing. Imogen led her into the stable then removed her blanket to show off her pure white coat. It was the smoothest, whitest hair imaginable. Where the winter sun touched it through the open door, it sparkled. She was the most stunning horse the girls had ever seen.

'This is Guinevere,' Imogen announced. 'You can stroke her gently, if you like.'

They certainly did like. Her coat was softer than velvet.

'Why the plume?' asked Alice. 'Has she been in a show?'

'Good gracious, no!' replied Imogen, laughing. 'She'd hate that. She has to wear it when she's above ground, unfortunately. Remember what I said, no shrieking please, this may come as rather a shock.'

Turning her back to the girls, she unfastened Guinevere's headdress, removed it carefully and stepped aside. Sarah stumbled backwards and managed to grasp a trough to prevent herself from falling over. Her eyes were wide and bulging. Alice gasped but then couldn't stop smiling.

'She's a unicorn!' she whispered.

'Indeed she is,' said Imogen. 'But no one else needs to know that, do they?' She stroked Guinevere's nose and replaced her headdress before getting the girls to stand next to her for a photograph. 'Smile!' she said needlessly, 'This one's to show Lucinda! Even with her horn covered, she will be the most beautiful creature she has encountered. You can tell her she belongs to you, Alice, but is in a secret location due to her value. That's not untrue, she belongs to all of us and she is priceless.'

'What if Lucinda wants to see her?'

'That's the whole idea. She'll be so desperate to see her, she'll do anything to be your friend, I'm sure. You'll just have to keep her waiting.'

'I see,' said Alice slowly, not exactly thrilled at the prospect of deceiving two members of the Rowbottom family.

'Brilliant!' enthused Sarah.

'I'll leave it to you to explain how you came to own her,' Imogen added. 'Back down to the village, then.'

The pixie-looking stable hand was replacing Guinevere's blanket as they waved goodbye from the lift.

'So, what's next on the agenda?' asked Alice as the doors closed.

'Whatever it is, it won't top that!' said Sarah, ecstatic about meeting a unicorn.

'You will have your robe fitted, Alice, while I print that picture,' replied Imogen. She led them back through the underground stables and along the corridor to the door labelled 'TAILOR AND FITTING ROOMS.' She knocked on the door and peeped inside. 'Here they are, Freya!' she announced, showing them in. 'I'll see you in a few minutes,' she said as she backed out of the door.

Freya introduced herself to Sarah as she scurried around the room as quickly as she could, gathering up the fabric that was strewn all over the place. 'Ooh, you're going to love this, Alice,' she said as she disappeared into a walk-in wardrobe. The girls chose two chairs from a row of half a dozen alongside an enormous mirror and sat down. There was an old-fashioned sewing machine on a table and several changing rooms with velvet curtains. Sarah was in raptures, her eyes trying to take in the detail of all the wonderful outfits hanging around the room.

'My sisters would be so jealous!' she whispered. Alice's thoughts were elsewhere, imagining what a double dose of Rowbottom revenge would involve.

Freya reappeared and breezed into a fitting room. 'I've left it in there for you, Alice,' she said. 'I hope you like it.'

'Thank you,' replied Alice, wandering in and closing the curtain behind her. It seemed Sarah was far more excited that she was. She could hear her feet tapping in anticipation, and Freya said,

'I'll make one for you as well. We can't have you wearing jeans when we've got special clothes, can we?'

'Will you, really?' asked Sarah, scarcely able to believe her luck. 'Thank you!'

After a few minutes of rustling fabric, Alice pulled back the curtain and emerged shyly from the fitting room. Sarah's mouth fell open. Even Freya was temporarily speechless. Alice turned to look in the mirror and barely knew herself. Gazing back at her was a girl who could easily be mistaken for a medieval princess. Not the awkward schoolgirl who was uncomfortable with her image, but the most striking girl she could wish to be. The long, powder-blue dress fitted perfectly and the beads on the bodice glittered in the dancing light of the lamps. It was made of the same remarkable fabric as Imogen's dress, only a different colour. Intricate swirls of silver embroidery and sparkling stones flashed on her navy blue velvet cloak as she stared, trying to take it all in.

'You look … magical,' confirmed Sarah, getting up to give her friend a hug.

'Thank you,' said Alice quietly. As far as she was concerned, this was a much better transformation than the wings. If only the coven could see her now.

'Do you like it?' asked Freya, wiping a tear from her eye.

'It's better than anything I ever imagined,' whispered Alice. 'Thank you so much.'

There was knock at the door and Imogen's face appeared.

'That's ... quite a transformation!' she exclaimed. 'You just need your wings, Alice.' She showed Alice a deep red bottle and removed the stopper. 'This method is not to be used very often. When you're ready, inhale once, OK?'

Alice leaned over the bottle and breathed in deeply. Her nose was filled with such an intense smell of fruit, flowers and cut grass, it almost knocked her off her feet. Imogen held her arm to steady her. Within seconds, her wings emerged, gliding easily through the slots in her dress and cloak. Alice wiped her brow with her hand – it always made her feel hot when that happened. She glanced at the mirror; now the image was complete. As her damp, transparent wings unfurled to their full size, everything suddenly looked right. Alice was clearly meant to be a Finwip, there was no mistake. Her wings lit up like stained glass as she turned her back to a lamp and faced the others.

'Perfect,' said Imogen. Freya and Sarah both had tears in their eyes now.

'Pull yourselves together!' said Imogen, smiling. 'Here's the photograph of Guinevere, Alice. DO NOT show anyone except Lucinda.'

'I won't,' said Alice solemnly.

'Now let's have some lunch! Enough surprises for one day.'

Neither Alice nor Sarah could argue with that.

*

Alice was amazed to find at least thirty other Finwips having lunch in the hall, including Thomas, who was just tucking in to an enormous slice of cake. Not the usual Thomas though. As they approached his table, Alice could see that he too was completely Finwip today, in his silver-grey robes with his Emperor dragonfly wings extending a long way out behind him. Anyone walking past had to do a detour to avoid walking in to them. Alice thought he looked much better as a Finwip. Even his long, dark, untidy hair somehow looked right in the overall picture now. He didn't look up from his food until they were standing directly in front of him.

'Oh ... my ... life! Is that really you, Wiglet?'

Alice grinned.

'Well, I'm ... flabbergasted. It's not often I'm stuck for words. You look great, Alice. Well done kiddo.'

'You look ... er ... better than usual as well. Funny, isn't it?'

'This is just who we are, simple as that.' He watched Sarah's expression as she tried to take everything in – so many people with various but beautiful wings, fascinating clothes and coloured hair, some tiny people, some with strangely shaped ears. And the most delicious-looking food laid out in front of the kitchen. 'You OK?' he asked. 'Sarah?'

She brought her gaze back to him. 'Thomas! You look so different, I didn't recognise you!' she said, embarrassed.

'Help yourself to some food,' he said, pointing to it. The girls wandered over to the buffet. They didn't know where to start. The kitchen staff had thoughtfully labelled the dishes: in the hot section was stuffed butternut squash or allotment pie (a vegetarian shepherd's pie). For dessert there was cherry plum flan, blackberry and orange cake, vanilla scones with damson jam or pineapple-halves filled with tropical fruit salad.

Sarah's face was a study when Fay asked them what they would like.

'Good to see you, Sarah! Is she keeping you on your toes?' she asked, glancing at Alice.

Sarah nodded. 'Um ... yes ... hello,' she mumbled. It was one of those occasions when, no matter how hard you try not to look at something, you can't stop yourself. Those pointed ears were incredible! Of course, she wasn't wearing a bandana today. Fay laughed.

'We'll have you looking like one of us soon!'

Sarah smiled, certain that she would much rather have wings than pointed ears. 'Are you all vegetarian here?' she asked, looking slightly disappointed.

'No,' replied Fay, 'but we need a lot more fruit and vegetables than normal humans. Would you prefer a bat meal?'

'Yuck! That sounds gross,' Sarah blurted out.

'It's not what it sounds like!' laughed Fay. 'It's just a meal with meat, for Finwips with bat wings. Not insect meat, though.'

'Oh, I see! No, thanks, I'll try some of this.' She took a portion of allotment pie. Alice chose the stuffed squash.

'How many puddings can we have?' she whispered to Fay.

'As many as you like, seeing as it's you!'

'Might have known you'd be eyeing up the desserts!' said a familiar voice over her shoulder. Her grandad was standing behind her.

'Grandad!' she shrieked. She stared in amazement at his golden robes and unusual, mottled wings with their ragged edge.

'You look a picture, Alice,' said her grandma proudly, appearing beside him. 'He doesn't scrub up too badly for an old'un, does he?'

Alice had to agree.

'I hope you're going to try my blackberry and orange cake, girls!' she continued. 'How are you coping with all this madness, Sarah? You sit next to me,' she insisted as they returned to Thomas's table. 'I'm normal, I can assure you.'

'That's good,' said Sarah gratefully. 'Although, I do love all this.'

'Me too,' admitted Grandma, giving her a hug.

Alice was struggling to eat her meal for all the compliments and welcoming comments she was receiving from other Finwips. She'd even had her photograph taken with some of them. When she had finally finished, she insisted that her grandad took one of her and Sarah – she wanted to make sure her friend didn't feel left out.

'We'll do another one when you get your robes,' she promised.

Sarah was looking forward to that. She sat back down next to Grandma. 'Do you think, after today, that I'll come here again?' she asked.

'I don't think you need to worry about that, my love,' she replied. 'I'm sure you'll be kept very busy in this community if I know Alice.'

Alice wasn't listening. Looking around at all the happy faces, she tried to picture how different the scene would be if the police suddenly stormed into the village. Or a group of scientists. At that moment she realised she couldn't let that happen. She would not let Brian Rowbottom destroy all this.

Chapter 9

Progress!

After an eventful day on Saturday, Alice took time out on Sunday morning to do normal things. Well, as normal as things could be for her given the circumstances. She hadn't done any harp practice for nearly a fortnight. She hadn't been in the mood for playing anyway, so it was a stroke of luck that her teacher, Miss Chambers, had been on holiday.

With Jack beside her, she took her seat next to her instrument in the corner of the dining room. This was the only room where there had been space for it. Her father complained at the time of its purchase, two years ago, that she should have stuck with the recorder. Small and inexpensive. Why had she chosen to play such a large instrument? All Alice knew was that she had been drawn to the sound of the harp. She took out the piece of music that she should have practised and pulled a face as she realised how long and complicated it was. She would never master that by Wednesday evening, it was too difficult. Reluctantly, she arranged the pages on her music stand and made a start. To her amazement, the music flowed easily. Her eyes could barely keep up with the notes on the page as her fingers played them so nimbly and smoothly. Jack sat up and wagged his tail as if enjoying the classical rendition. Alice kept going, not even needing to turn the pages, as she already seemed to know the piece by heart, though she had only heard it once when her teacher had played it to her. When the piece ended she sat back and smiled. The sound of clapping behind her made her jump and she turned to see her parents standing in the doorway, where they had been listening to her captivating performance.

'That was beautiful, Alice,' said her mother. 'The best I've heard you play.'

'Fantastic. Well done you! I think Miss Chambers will be pleasantly surprised!' added her father.

Alice blushed. 'Er, thanks,' she said awkwardly. 'Wasn't as difficult as I thought.'

As further practice was clearly unnecessary, Alice decided to move on to the kitchen and try out some of the Finwip recipes she had been given. She started with the banana and sultana crumble that the dinner lady had recommended. Lining a shallow dish with four sliced bananas, she felt her face turning red again at the thought of *that* incident at school. Would she always be traumatised by bananas now? She added a generous handful of plump sultanas and a few orange segments. Then she made the crumble topping, adding plenty of cinnamon. Judging by the muffled giggles coming from the lounge, Thomas must be making wise cracks about her culinary enterprise.

Soon the house was filled with the mouth-watering aroma of warm fruit and cinnamon. Thomas and Jack were waiting impatiently, peering through the oven door to see what was cooking. Her parents had forgotten their jokes and were also hovering to see what smelled so good. Alice put on some thick oven gloves and carefully removed her *chef d'oeuvre* from the oven. It looked and smelled delicious.

Thomas held up a large serving spoon. 'Don't be shy with my portion!' he instructed.

'Who said I'm sharing?' retorted Alice.

'They did!' he replied, waving the spoon at their parents.

Alice grimaced. She really had wanted it all to herself.

'Well, I am impressed, Alice!' exclaimed her mother, examining the crumble. 'What's come over you today? Is this dessert for this evening?'

'Actually it's lunch, I'm starving,' replied Alice bluntly.

'Glad you said that!' said her father, taking some bowls out of the cupboard.

Aaargh! Families! Alice was so annoyed she could have screamed. The crumble went down a treat with everyone, though she would have liked seconds and ideally, thirds. She would have licked the empty dish if Jack hadn't got there first.

That afternoon she took Jack for a walk to clear her head. Although her domestic efforts had been a distraction, the task of befriending Lucinda and ultimately rescuing a respected Finwip from the castle was still filling her with dread. She told Thomas she was going and sneaked out while her parents were having their Sunday afternoon nap. Trudging down the road with the snow squeaking beneath her boots, Alice felt better for being out of the house. She just couldn't relax at home knowing that she was keeping such a secret from her parents and always having to guard against letting anything slip out. Thomas had been doing it for years. Perhaps leading a double life would get easier as time went on. He didn't even know what his Finwip ability was yet. Perhaps the future held an even bigger challenge for him.

'Oh, Jack, why can't life be simple?' she muttered. Jack looked up at her and smiled. Or was he just panting? Alice could see his hot breath in the air. 'As if you can understand me,' said Alice, giving herself a ticking off for trying to start a philosophical conversation with a dog. Jack barked.

'Well, can you?' He barked again, wagging his tail.

'I'm not convinced,' laughed Alice, unsure whether she was talking to Jack or herself. He began to pull on the lead as they approached the old oak tree at the end of the road. Next to the oak and its mysterious letterbox, which still looked real enough to Alice, was an alleyway between two houses which joined a path to the woods. Jack evidently wanted to go that way but Alice didn't fancy it on her own. It would be dark in about half an hour.

As she pulled him away and turned to go back the way they came, he spotted two birds very close to them. He sat down on the spot and watched them. Alice was convinced they were the same blackbird and robin who had followed her to school recently. Only this time, it wasn't their friendly behaviour that intrigued her – it was the fact they were perched on the Finwip letterbox again. She now knew that meant it was real to them as well. Jack stood up on his hind legs to get a closer look at these cheeky birds. To Alice's amazement, he leant his front paws on the letterbox. Finwip 'magic' must be seen by all animals, she deduced. The birds appeared to have no fear of her or Jack as they stared back into the huge face of her curious dog.

'Come on, let's go,' insisted Alice, patting his back. He jumped down and did as he was told. Remarkable. Perhaps he could understand her after all! As they walked leisurely back up Albany Road, the two birds followed in their usual manner, flitting from hedge to gatepost, chirping as they went. A squirrel racing up the trunk of a birch tree stopped to stare at them as they passed by. Alice began to wonder if she had stumbled onto the set of a children's film. 'Don't be silly,' she told herself sternly, shaking her head. When she arrived at her own gate, the birds gave a final chirp and flew away. Jack barked goodbye.

'Never a dull moment,' said Alice under her breath as she let herself in. She couldn't even walk the dog without a strange occurrence.

*

At school on Monday, Alice started to put the plan into place. Since Saturday she had felt different, more confident, and was determined to play her part in helping the Finwip community. She began by giving Christmas cards to the coven. Katy raised an eyebrow and tossed hers aside after opening it. Sarah gave them a card each as well, to Alice's amusement.

'It can only help,' she said. Lucinda felt rather disconcerted.

'Er, Sarah,' she began, turning round in her seat. 'I'm sorry about the cake incident. And you, Alice.' She was flushed with embarrassment, aware that Katy and Olivia were listening in horror to her apology.

'I'm sorry too,' said Alice, forcing her best convincing smile. 'Shall we call it quits?'

Lucinda nodded and turned away quickly.

Sarah made a thumbs-up gesture in her lap. Alice gave a nod of acknowledgement. She handed Sarah a bag containing a fruit and cereal slice she had made on Sunday evening.

'One of your special recipes?' she asked.

'Of course. It's not bad, actually.'

'Let's hope it stops you snacking in art lessons.'

Alice stuck her tongue out.

*

Frustratingly, it wasn't until Wednesday, the last day of term, that she really made progress with Lucinda. Geography passed without a hitch. Alice didn't answer any questions and spent most of the lesson staring at a map of the world on the wall, trying to guess the locations of all the Finwip villages. At break she found Lucinda sitting in a corner of the cloakroom trying to do her French homework before the lesson. She had been told off the previous lesson for turning up without it, so would be in serious trouble this time.

'Need any help?' Alice asked.

Lucinda looked up, surprised at her offer. 'Er, if you don't mind,' she replied awkwardly. 'You know I'm rubbish at French.'

Alice sat down next to her and, as Lucinda went through the comprehension questions, Alice pointed to the sentence in the passage where she could find the answer. Lucinda scribbled down the last answer with five minutes of break time to spare.

'Thank you,' she said earnestly. 'I owe you one.'

'You like horses, don't you?' said Alice, pretending to be naive. 'What do you think of this one?' She pulled the photo of Guinevere from the inner pocket of her blazer. Lucinda's eyes opened wide as she looked at the photo.

'It's … incredible!' she exclaimed. 'I've never seen a horse quite like it. Whose is it?'

'She's mine,' replied Alice calmly.

'No way! What breed is she? Where did you get her from? She must have cost a fortune!'

'I don't know what breed she is. Very rare, I'm told. It's a long story, but it was a surprise, which had something to do with my grandfather. And yes, I believe she is quite valuable. I don't know a lot about horses, it's all new to me.'

'You don't even ride, do you?'

'Er, no. I'll learn, though.'

For the first time ever, Lucinda looked at Alice enviously. 'Can I see her?' she asked.

'Not for a while I'm afraid,' explained Alice, just as Imogen had advised her. 'She's being looked after by friends at the moment. She's very nervous and wary of strangers.'

'Oh, that is a shame,' said Lucinda, visibly disappointed. 'Maybe soon, then.'

'I'll see what I can do,' fibbed Alice.

When the bell sounded, she joined Sarah and Sebastian, who were walking upstairs to the French room. She caught the tail end of their conversation.

'So, why are you and Alice talking to Lucinda and Co?' Sebastian queried. 'I thought you couldn't stand them.'

'Er, good question,' replied Sarah, trying to think of a sensible answer. 'I think Alice would rather be friends than enemies. She's had enough of their comments lately.'

'I can understand that,' conceded Sebastian, suddenly aware that Alice was behind him. 'Are you alright today?' he asked.

'Oh, fine thank you,' she replied, touched by his consideration.

'Sometimes my mum has a funny turn like yours,' he went on. 'They never last long though.'

'Thank goodness,' said Alice, grinning in the knowledge that Sebastian's mum's 'turns' couldn't be anything like hers.

During the lesson, Lucinda was praised by Mme Péraud not only for completing her homework, but for answering the questions correctly. She grinned at Alice. Katy and Olivia were evidently not so happy and cast several dirty looks in Alice's direction, betraying their jealousy. Lucinda didn't seem to care. The truth was she was preoccupied with that horse in the photograph and would do anything to see it.

Later on, in maths, Alice was sailing confidently through the excercise they had been set, unaware that the rest of the class had been looking at each other uncomfortably for five minutes or so. Mrs Myers hadn't explained the principles clearly enough. A few more examples wouldn't have gone amiss for most of the class. The teacher soon realised her error, but was quick to point out that Alice was not experiencing any problems. The first Alice knew of this was when she felt the rest of the room turning to stare at her. However, this time was different. When Lucinda just smiled, the rest of the coven did the same, grudgingly. Then no one else dared say anything derogatory and simply looked away. Sarah raised her eyebrows in surprise.

'Bonus!' whispered Alice. It seemed being nice to Lucinda may have more than one positive outcome.

After school, Alice started to walk home and passed Lucinda sitting on the wall outside, waiting for her mother.

'Just the person,' she grinned, getting up. 'Would you like to come to my house and learn to ride?' she asked.

'Really? Yes, please, that would be great!'

'I'll check with my mum, but how about ten o'clock tomorrow morning, first day of the holidays?'

'Sounds fine, thanks,' said Alice, trying to sound calm. She smiled gratefully and carried on walking. Whilst being overjoyed at her progress, she was also terrified by the thought of meeting Brian. Further down the road, a horn sounded and Alice saw Lucinda and her mother waving at her from a red Porsche. She waved back enthusiastically.

Amazing, thought Alice. All this because she thinks I've got something she hasn't. Imagine if she really knew …

Chapter 10

An Invitation

The sound of that same loud horn alerted Alice to the arrival of Lucinda and Mrs Rowbottom on Thursday morning. Thomas looked out of his window and saw the Porsche.

'You lucky cow!' he called to Alice as she galloped down the stairs and grabbed her warmest coat and gloves. 'Does Lucinda have an older sister, by any chance?'

'Yes, actually,' Alice replied before slamming the front door in her haste.

Lucinda got out of the car to let Alice climb into the back. The smell of new leather was still strong, even though competing with expensive perfume.

'Good morning, Alice,' said Mrs Rowbottom cheerfully. 'Looking forward to your riding lesson?'

'Oh yes, very much,' gushed Alice, making a special effort to be polite, while trying not to stare at all the gold necklaces that must be weighing down Mrs Rowbottom's neck. She wondered how she could grip the steering wheel wearing so many rings. Her bleached blonde hair was perfectly styled with so much hairspray that Alice suspected it would crack if she tapped it.

'You'll be fine,' assured Lucinda. 'I've chosen our best pony for you.'

'Thanks,' said Alice. She felt rather stupid in her jeans and thick waterproof jacket. Lucinda was wearing a black coat edged with fake black fur over her riding gear, looking every bit as though they were going to a fashion show rather than a muddy field.

'Don't worry,' said Lucinda, as if sensing her awkwardness. 'I've got some riding clothes ready for you at home, you can change when we get there.'

Alice smiled in appreciation, already feeling cramped in the small space she had in the back of the car. No better than her mum's Mini, really.

Fortunately they were there in ten minutes. Alice couldn't decide if she was more excited or nervous.

The electric gates opened when Lucinda pressed the remote. Mrs Rowbottom parked the Porsche in one of the garages, just as Grandad had seen. The house was magnificent, even from the outside. It had timbered gables, leaded windows, several balconies and a tennis court to the front. Inside, Alice stared out of the window at the garden. The Rowbottoms had their own lake with a pedalo, canoes and a motorboat. In the distance, she could see a horse, so the field and stables must be further down.

'I've left the clothes in a changing room for you,' said Lucinda. 'I'll show you.'

Changing rooms in a house? Oh, of course. For the indoor swimming pool. Alice had to smile when she saw the pool had its own kitchen area and bar for entertaining.

'You must have some fantastic parties here!' she enthused.

'We do! But not this Christmas, my dad has decided to have the big party at the castle this year.'

'Oh, I did see something in the paper about him buying the castle,' Alice admitted, trying not to sound too interested.

'I'll wait for you outside,' said Lucinda.

Alice got changed as quickly as possible, squeezing into Lucinda's clothes, which were unpleasantly tight. At least the boots fitted properly. She took the hat with her and joined Lucinda to walk down to the paddock. It seemed silly, wasting time learning to ride when she was unlikely to get on a horse again after today. Lucinda proved to be a good teacher, though. It certainly helped that Blaze, the pony Alice was riding, was very well trained and responded to all commands. Alice found it quite easy, trotting alongside Lucinda on her pony and, to her surprise, she was enjoying it.

'I've never seen Blaze so well-behaved!' said Lucinda. 'She seems to like you!'

Mmm. Another animal that appeared to understand her. She would have to ask Imogen about this. Perhaps she was imagining it. But then again, until last week, she thought she had imagined someone at her window. 'Er, yes, she does,' murmured Alice, unsure what else to say. At least her cheeks blushing in embarrassment wouldn't be noticed beneath the red glow of the cold. She looked back up the garden at the house. 'This really is a dream home,' she said. 'You're so lucky to live here.'

'Oh, I know, we do love it. You're welcome to come again, if you like.'

'Thank you!' Lucinda was actually a decent person, it seemed. Not at all like she was at school, with the coven. Unless all this was just an act because she was desperate to see Guinevere. Perhaps she was as cunning as her father. That thought put Alice back on track with her mission.

'Is your dad working at the castle, then?'

'Yes,' said Lucinda, pulling a face. 'He's hardly been at home since he bought it. I don't know what he's doing there, but he's been working until late at night. I suppose he prefers to work after closing time, when there are no tourists.'

'Perhaps,' agreed Alice, relieved that she wasn't going to bump into him today. There was still a chance that Theo may be at the house, though. But surely Lucinda's mother would know every inch of her home, so there would be nowhere to hide him?

'What's that small building for at the end of the drive?' asked Alice. 'Sorry, I don't mean to be nosey,' she added hurriedly.

'By the gates? That's the old lodge. Dad uses it as an office for his property business. His PA works in there and there are people coming and going all the time. Evenings and weekends too.'

'He must be very busy,' commented Alice, intrigued.

'Oh, I don't think it's *all* about work,' continued Lucinda. 'We see people taking in food, drink and all sorts of things with them. But Mum, Isabella and I are never invited to whatever goes on in there. We don't care, though, it must get pretty cramped, it's only small. Shall we leave the riding there for today and have some lunch? You've done really well for a first lesson.'

'Sounds good to me,' replied Alice. 'I've learned a lot, thanks.' She really had. Could the lodge be the entrance to the underground Sinwip village? All those people going in to such a small building at any time of day? Lucinda, as well as her mum and sister, clearly had no idea what was going on. Perhaps it was better that way.

They got changed out of their riding clothes and met up back in the kitchen. Mrs Rowbottom had left lunch ready for them. In the fridge Lucinda found a selection of small sandwiches and on the table was a cake box from a bakery Alice hadn't heard of. Lucinda lifted the lid.

'I asked mum to get this for you,' she explained. 'I suppose I should have invited Sarah as well. It was her cake I ruined at the sale.'

She slid the box along the table to Alice, who was thrilled to find a splendid cake, decorated with glazed fresh fruit and piled high with berries.

'Wow!' she exclaimed, Lucinda's generosity taking her by surprise. 'You needn't have bought this! But thank you, it looks wonderful.'

'I noticed you seem to like fruit!' said Lucinda.

'Er … yes,' admitted Alice. 'I have been eating a lot of it lately. My mum has been making us eat healthy food at home.'

'Well, it can't be doing any harm, you seem to be getting brainier!'

'Ha, yes, it must be all the vitamins!' laughed Alice, trying to make a joke of it. As they ate lunch, she changed the subject to Christmas, keen to steer the conversation away from her own recent behaviour. Lucinda had already been shopping for presents with her sister. 'Did you buy anything exciting?' asked Alice politely.

'No, not really. But I did get a brilliant outfit for the Christmas ball. It's a red dress with a black hooded cloak. I got a mask too.'

'A mask?'

'It's a medieval masquerade ball this year, since it's being held in a medieval castle,' clarified Lucinda.

'It sounds amazing,' cooed Alice, cutting her cake. 'Have a slice, at least,' she insisted.

'OK, thanks. I'll be back in a minute.'

Lucinda left the table and disappeared upstairs. She returned with a rolled up paper.

'For you and Sarah,' she announced, handing it over with a smile.

Alice took what turned out to be a scroll tied with red ribbon. She unrolled it carefully and realised that this parchment-style paper was an invitation. Hardly daring to believe her luck, she read:

You and a guest are invited to

The Medieval Masquerade Ball

at Aylesford Castle
on Saturday 21ˢᵗ December.

As friends of the Rowbottom family you will be treated to an evening of festive fun and indulgence in the most magnificent setting.

Guaranteed to be an unforgettable experience.

7.30pm till late. Masks obligatory!

R.S.V.P.

Brian, Jacqueline, Isabella and Lucinda

This was what the village had been waiting for. Alice was now that 'unique someone' that her grandad had spoken of. A Finwip as well as a friend of the Rowbottoms.

'I don't know what to say!' she gasped eventually. 'Thank you so much! Sarah will be so pleased when I tell her. Oh wow! This means we've only got two days to find something to wear!'

Alice was really thinking that an outfit was the least of her concerns. She needed to tell Imogen immediately and find out exactly what the plan was once she arrived at the party. That feeling of excitement mixed with fear was now stronger than ever.

'Don't panic,' Lucinda reassured her. 'A long dress and a mask are all you need. The costume shop in town has a whole range of masks. It will be fun, you'll see. Dad's planning an extra special one this year.'

Bet I know why, thought Alice. 'I can't wait!' she said.

As soon as Mrs Rowbottom had driven her home, Alice raced upstairs to bang on Thomas's door. A sleepy-looking head appeared.

'I've done it,' she said proudly, 'I've got an invitation to the ball at the castle! Sarah is invited too.'

'You jammy thing!' said Thomas. 'That's great, though. We need to let the village know so they can start making plans.'

'We're going to need costumes,' said Alice, worried. It's a medieval theme. Do you think Freya can help? There's not much time before Saturday night.'

'I'm sure something can be sorted. Listen, I'll go and let them know. You can give Sarah the good news. I think she deserves a treat for putting up with you!'

Alice opened her mouth to say something rude, but stopped herself. He had a point.

'See if she can come over tomorrow,' suggested Thomas. 'We've got a lot to organise.'

ALICE PARKER'S METAMORPHOSIS

By late afternoon, everything was arranged. Sarah's sister would bring her over in the morning, then she, Alice and Thomas would go down to Finwip village to discuss the task ahead. Alice still couldn't imagine how she would find and rescue someone in a huge castle with so many people around. Still, a few days ago she never dreamed she would grow wings or be invited to a Rowbottom Christmas extravaganza …

Chapter 11

The Best Laid Plans

Alice had never seen Sarah so excited. For one who was usually calm, she could hardly keep still, she was so thrilled about the party at the castle. As soon as her sister had driven off, she began her happy ramblings. 'I never ever dreamed I'd be invited to one of the Rowbottom's parties. You really have excelled yourself this time, Alice. And I don't mean that in a sarcastic way, for once. It's unbelievable. First my best friend grows wings, then she takes me to an amazing secret village and now the ultimate Christmas ball! So much has happened in such a short space of time! Life doesn't get much better than this, surely?'

'Glad you're enjoying it,' said Alice dryly, standing in the hall with her arms folded.

'Oh ... sorry, I didn't think. I'm so looking forward to the party, I almost forgot the real reason we're going.'

'Shame I can't. Are you ready to go, Thomas?' she called up the stairs impatiently.

'On my way!' he shouted, slamming his bedroom door and hurrying down. 'Good job the folks aren't here,' he said as he put on his coat. 'We don't have to make up a story as to where the three of us are going. Mind you, you'll have some explaining to do, Alice, if Mum realises how much you've eaten for breakfast again.'

'She'll think it was you.'

'Why?'

'I didn't clean up the mess I made.'

'Charming.'

They stepped out into the winter sunshine for a brisk walk down to the oak tree. Thomas and Sarah chatted about Christmas parties, while Alice was racked with guilt in the knowledge that she had deceived Lucinda. She wasn't a bad person. Not only that, but worse was still to come. How could she smile at her at the ball, then try to find the man her father had kidnapped? It was hard to believe that someone could be held captive where a party was taking place. Twisted, in fact. She rubbed her eyes as if hoping it would help her see the situation more clearly. All she knew was that she had a responsibility to help the village and to protect the secret existence of Finwips all over the world. When they arrived at the tree lift, Alice and Sarah went first, while Thomas waited outside to follow. Alice was silent.

'You look worried,' Sarah commented as they travelled down.

'Wouldn't you be, in my shoes?'

'Probably. But don't forget, you won't be alone, you'll have me with you. Whatever the plan is, they won't want to put you in *real* danger, will they? You seem to be very important to them.'

'I suppose so,' replied Alice, sounding unconvinced. Was she? Or did they just want Theo back, whatever it took?

When Thomas joined them, they made their way along the corridor to the dining hall, where they could hear muffled voices already. On entering, they realised that the voices were coming from a small meeting room to the right-hand side of the main room. There was a group, including their grandad, sitting at a long table with Imogen standing at one end. She turned to greet them.

'Welcome, come and sit down,' she said with a business-like efficiency. 'Congratulations Alice, on what you have achieved for us already. This morning, with your help, we're going to confirm a plan to finally rescue Theo.'

Alice nodded and forced a smile. She took the empty seat next to her grandad, while Sarah and Thomas sat further along.

'This is Theo's daughter, Anna,' Imogen added.

She waved her hand towards a lady with shoulder-length black hair, who was sitting at the opposite end of the table. She was noticeably pale and looked exhausted, with dark rings under her eyes. Alice felt sorry for her immediately.

'I'm very grateful to you all,' said Anna quietly. 'Especially you, Alice. I've heard good things about you.'

'Er, thank you,' said Alice, unsure how to respond. She began to feel more nervous as she realised just how much people were pinning their hopes on her. Her grandad squeezed her hand.

'Now,' continued Imogen, 'as you all know, the party takes place at the castle tomorrow evening, so we haven't much time to prepare ourselves. Alice and Sarah will be attending as guests.' She turned to the girls. 'Freya is currently working on your outfits. Dresses, cloaks and masks in dark colours will be best – I have suggested black and navy blue.' Sarah smiled, nodding in agreement.

'You will also have velvet bags in which to carry torches, food and a party costume for Theo. You will need to take fruit and juice for him. He may be lacking energy. He will not be easy for two young girls to support if he is struggling to walk.'

Now Sarah looked worried. The gravity of their task was only just beginning to sink in. Alice raised her hand as if at school.

'How do I know where to look for him? The castle is so vast, I wouldn't know where to start.'

'I can help you there,' said Grandad. 'I've spent days there with my OAP annual pass and I've been watching Rowbottom's movements carefully. He has been going to the South Tower at least three times a day, taking a brown paper bag with him and leaving without it. I'm pretty sure Theo is in there.'

'What if there's another reason for Brian to go to that tower?' asked Alice.

'I can't think of one. It hasn't been in use since the fire three years ago. It destroyed a couple of floors quite high up in the tower and rather than go to the expense of restoring it, the previous owners simply closed it to the public. As far I can tell there's nothing wrong with the other floors.'

'And what happens if I *do* get recognised as a Finwip? What will Brian do?'

There was a tension-laden silence. Grandad took a deep breath. 'Firstly, that won't happen. You cannot possibly be detected until twelve months after your wings emerge. Secondly, we only know of two other Finwips who have been caught by Brian. And they're still with us.'

'But what happened to them?' persisted Alice.

'They were locked up and deprived of food until they revealed their ability. Neither of them proved useful to him, so he humiliated them for a while in front of his Sinwip cronies, then demanded a ransom for their release. We had to pay. Unfortunately, Theo is too valuable to let go. Somehow Rowbottom knew about his ability – this is the first time he has plucked one of us off the street. There's no doubt, a brain like yours would be a great asset to him. I don't want to think about how he'd use it.'

Sarah and Thomas had turned pale. All eyes were on Alice, who was biting her bottom lip.

'Fair enough,' she said, after a few seconds. 'Though I can't see him doing that to a friend of Lucinda's. We'll see, won't we?' She shrugged her shoulders. Grandad patted her on the back and nodded to Imogen to carry on.

She handed out copies of a map of the castle. 'We have these courtesy of Daniel here, who works on the maintenance team.' This must be the Finwip they had mentioned before, who was virtually impossible to detect. Daniel removed his green cap with the Aylesford Castle emblem embroidered in gold and bowed his head to everyone, revealing his small, pointed ears.

'This is my bunch of keys,' he said hesitantly, looking at Alice. 'They're all labelled. This one is to the South Tower,' he said, pointing to a very large, rusty one. The internal doors shouldn't be locked, there's nothing in there worth protecting. Please keep these keys safe, I could lose my job if I'm found out.'

'Oh, I will, I promise,' vowed Alice as she accepted them.

Her grandad leaned over to explain the map. 'As you can see, the difficulty lies in getting from the dining hall or ball room, where the party is being held, to the South Tower, without drawing attention to yourselves.'

Alice nodded. Thomas and Sarah looked at each other, raising an eyebrow.

'The best way will be to walk around the outside of the building. Trying to access it from inside will be far too complicated and involve too many locked doors and alarms. The external door to the tower is here,' he pointed out, marking it with his pencil. 'That's the one with the large key. Once inside, you will need to check several floors as quickly as you can. Just open every door and call his name, no one else should be in there. Chances are, if you find a locked door, that's where he is. Let's hope you have the key on that bunch.'

'OK,' said Alice, fiddling nervously with the keys.

'Once you have offered him something to eat and drink, you must get him to change into the party costume immediately, so that he won't look out of place as you pass back through. When you leave the castle via the main entrance, you need to turn right and make your way across the grass to the river, there will be two boats waiting.'

'We're getting out of there by boat?'

'It's the best option. There will be no access for vehicles, even visitor car parks are far away from the main building. On the night, guests will be dropped off at the end of the drive and taken up to the castle by horse and cart.'

Alice frowned. 'I don't like the idea of walking out of the front door. What if someone is standing there, a porter or security guard? They're bound to ask where we're going.'

'That has crossed my mind,' admitted Grandad. 'If someone asks, you say that your grandad, who will be Theo, has had too much to drink and needs some air. They won't argue if they think someone might be sick on a tapestry!'

Alice shook her head in disbelief at her real grandad's questionable logic and audacity.

'Allow me to introduce Jake and Ethan,' Imogen continued, nodding towards two young men at the table who had been silent so far. 'They are experienced rowers and will be able to get you away as fast as possible.' They nodded emphatically.

'Thomas, you and I will be waiting in the boats as well,' Grandad informed him. 'On standby, just in case.'

'Good idea,' agreed Thomas.

'How far will we be going by boat?' asked Sarah, not relishing the idea of being in a rowing boat in the dark at all.

'Not too far, don't worry,' Imogen reassured her. 'Just as far as the nearest car park, where Fay and I will be waiting with a van large enough to transport us all.'

'Are you sure you're going to be alright with this?' Anna asked Alice. She obviously had misgivings.

'Oh, yes, we'll be fine,' said Alice, lying through her teeth. She was far from sure, but how could she say anything else to this poor woman? 'I'll do everything I can to find your dad, I promise.'

'Of course she will,' added Grandad. 'She's a tough nut, this one. And she'll have a good friend with her, as well as us waiting in the wings. We'll make a good team.' He put his arm around her and roughed up her hair. She cringed with embarrassment.

'Thank you,' said Anna. 'I'll be there as well but I won't get in the way.'

'Well, everyone, is there anything else?' asked Imogen.

'Yes,' said Grandad. 'I trust we shall be having our Christmas party once Theo is back with us? We could all do with a celebration when this is over.'

'Absolutely! We'll make it the best yet – it will be Alice's first one too!' grinned Imogen.

There was a knock and a very tired Freya put her head round the door.

'Just to let you know, girls, your outfits will be ready in the morning if you want to collect them.'

They thanked her before she disappeared.

'Thank you for coming, everyone,' said Imogen. 'I'll see you all tomorrow evening. Get a good night's sleep tonight and good luck.'

'You won't need luck, you'll do fine,' professed Grandad, giving Alice a hug before they left. 'See you on the river!'

'I'm going to stay here for a while,' said Thomas. 'I'll see you two back at home.'

Alice smiled, putting on a brave face.

'Come on you,' said Sarah, taking her arm and leading her out. 'Enough serious talk. We've got the rest of the day to do as we please.'

Alice wasn't really in the mood for enjoying herself. As everyone left the meeting room, she signalled to Sarah to wait while she stayed behind to ask Imogen a question.

'Er … Imogen,' she began apprehensively.

'What is it, Alice?' she asked. 'Don't be shy, you can talk to me about anything that is bothering you.'

'Well, this may be a silly question. Ridiculous, really … but I've been meaning to ask you if animals can understand Finwips,' Alice blurted out, blushing.

Sarah stared at her friend fearing that she had finally lost the plot. Imogen seemed shocked.

'Has something happened to make you think so? Which animal was involved?'

'My dog, a couple of birds and possibly a horse,' replied Alice.

Sarah tried to stifle a giggle.

Imogen sat back down at the table, stunned. Alice thought that if she carried a hip flask like her grandad, now would be the time to offer it.

'Well,' said Imogen slowly. 'It has been known, but I must stress that it is a very rare ability. We used to have a Finwip elder called Ruby who could be understood and sometimes even protected by animals. Wild birds would often follow her to keep her company.'

Alice bit her lip again. Sarah decided that she needed to sit down as well.

'If that is what you are experiencing, Alice, you are even more extraordinary than we thought,' admitted Imogen. 'I need to carry out some more research into that. You are exhibiting incredibly strong characteristics for a new generation Finwip. Logically, traits and abilities should be disappearing, but you are reversing that.'

'I see,' murmured Alice. She was surprised but also relieved. More evidence that she wasn't going mad. 'Thank you, Imogen,' she said. 'We should go now Sarah.'

'You're welcome. Listen, you need to acquaint yourself with that map, Alice. And remember, whatever happens tomorrow night, stay calm. Make sure you carry your spray with you,' warned Imogen.

'I will,' pledged Alice. 'I mean, I'll try my best. Oh, no, I hadn't even thought of THAT happening! I've been so worried about being able to find Theo and get him out of there, the wings hadn't even crossed my mind! I must stay calm, otherwise I could ruin everything, couldn't I?'

'You could, that's true,' replied Imogen. 'But I know you won't. You have Sarah as a calming influence and I have every faith in you both.'

Alice looked down at the floor. She could hardly bear to look anyone in the eye at the moment, she was so doubtful of her capacity to do this.

'I don't want to let anyone down,' she said woefully, 'but I'm really not sure you've chosen the right person for the job.'

'I'm aware that this is asking a lot from a thirteen-year-old, but you really are our best chance. We had hoped that *you* would manage to get an invitation, but to have your friend there as well will be invaluable.'

'But how will we know when to slip away and search for him?'

'When you are least likely to be missed. I can't tell you when that will be, I'll leave it to your discretion, though I should think it will be after dinner. Don't leave the table if you can help it. That would be too obvious.'

'OK,' said Alice, resigning herself to the fact that she couldn't wriggle out of it.

'Try and enjoy yourself for part of the evening at least. Some people would give their right arm to be going to that ball!'

At that moment Alice would have given her right arm not to be going.

'I'll make sure she does,' Sarah promised her. 'I certainly intend to make the most of it.'

'Good,' said Imogen. 'Now, go and relax, save your energy for tomorrow night. Remember, you'll need to be alert at all times, so no sneaky glass of champagne!'

The girls smiled, said their goodbyes and headed off down the corridor.

'I love this place,' said Sarah, looking around as they waited for the lift. 'Don't you?'

'Mmm. I just hope I see it again after tomorrow.'

Chapter 12

Fireworks at the Castle

Thomas knocked loudly on Alice's bedroom door.

'Come in if you must,' replied a grouchy, sleepy voice.

'This just isn't good enough!' he complained, marching in and opening the curtains. 'It's nearly ten o'clock! While you've been snoring, I've been down to the village and collected your outfits for tonight.'

'Ooh, let's see!' piped up Sarah, jumping out of bed and putting on her dressing gown.

'Listen,' said Thomas lowering his voice, 'I've told Mum and Dad that a friend of mine made these for you, OK?'

'OK.'

'Fine.'

'This is yours, Sarah,' he said, passing her a large silver bag. 'And this one is yours.'

He laid the second bag in front of Alice, on her bed. She stared at it, but didn't touch it. Sarah had already opened hers and was squealing as she pulled out the dress and held it up.

Alice remained sitting up in bed, her arms folded.

'Calm down, Alice, you're over-excited again,' joked Thomas.

She scowled at him.

'It's alright for her,' she moaned, nodding in Sarah's direction, 'wetting herself about new outfits. I can't get excited about the party. I'm too worried.'

'Oh, give it a rest! Look at it like this: you're going to an amazing event and while you're there, you're going to collect someone. That's it. You're doing nothing wrong; they are.'

Alice sighed and dragged her fingers through her morning bird's-nest hair. 'Well, when you put it like that ...' Eventually she reached for the bag and took out her dress.

'I must admit, it's very nice.'

'NICE?' challenged Sarah, wide-eyed. 'I've never seen anything like them!'

'I know, I know … you're right,' Alice agreed. 'Freya's done a great job. You can clear off now, Thomas, so we can try these on.'

'Oh, will that be all for today, m'lady? No, of course not, madam will require a lift this evening,' said Thomas, before leaving the room with a bow. Sarah giggled.

'Don't flatter him,' snapped Alice.

'You're not very nice to him, are you? He's good to you.'

'He never used to be. He only changed when he realised I was becoming one of *them.*'

'Whatever, you'd have been in a right mess without his help.'

Alice shrugged her shoulders. 'Let's try these on quickly, I need to spend some time studying that map today.'

Needless to say, Alice had tried hers on and wolfed down some breakfast before Sarah managed to tear herself away from the mirror.

'Blimey,' remarked Alice, as she came back into her bedroom. 'Would you like some more time alone with the mirror, or has it confirmed that you are the fairest of them all?'

'Give over!' said Sarah, blushing. 'I'm admiring the clothes, not myself.'

'Mum asked if we were going out today. I said no, too much to do for this evening.'

'Really? That sounds boring. Surely it won't take all day to learn the layout of the castle?'

'Can't be too careful,' replied Alice.

'What will happen, will happen,' said Sarah as she hung her dress on the back of the door.

'Ooh, the voice of reason has spoken.'

'Yes, it has and you know it's right.'

'Fine, let's concentrate on it until lunch time, then we'll take the afternoon off.'

'Agreed. Did you leave any breakfast for me?'

'Cheeky cow.' Alice took out the map and laid it on her desk while Sarah went downstairs. She marked with a pencil the entrance, the Great Hall where the banquet would take place, and the ballroom. To get from there to the South Tower would mean walking along the back of the main building and passing many windows. She hoped that their dark cloaks and masks would be sufficient to blend into the darkness. Would CCTV be able to see much at night? She hadn't been to the castle for a couple of years, but as far as she could remember, there were no trees on that side of the Inner Court which they could hide behind. She studied the map closely. They knew about the door into the tower from the courtyard, but there was no door on the other side of the tower to get outside the castle wall. Alice didn't fancy walking back through the party, even if Theo was in costume. He'd probably still look dreadful after his ordeal. But they needed to get out via the Great Hall. She took out her ruler. If the scale on the map were correct, the tower itself was only 30m away from the river. Surely it would be simpler to escape through a ground floor window? They would have to scramble across the dry moat, though. That would be no mean feat wearing long dresses and helping an old man – and they might still be caught. Alice couldn't think of anything worse than being deprived of food at the moment ...

'Have you sorted it all out yet?' asked Sarah, appearing with a plateful of breakfast.

'I think there are two possible options,' replied Alice. 'But I'm not sure which one's worse. Are you up for climbing out of a window?'

'If I must.'

'We need to get past so many windows without being seen, I just don't know how we'll manage it.'

'Well, let's leave it until as late as possible. The more people have had to drink, the less likely they are to take any notice of what's going on outside. Or who's missing.'

'Good point,' said Alice, stealing a piece of toast with honey.

She talked Sarah through the map, showing her both escape routes.

'Mmm, I see what you mean,' said Sarah, wrinkling her nose. 'I think I prefer your grandad's suggestion. Anyway, I'm going to start packing my bag. Are you going to raid the fruit bowl when your parents go out?'

'That's the plan.'

'Excellent. That's the boring bit over, then. Put the telly on!'

Sarah busied herself with her bag while watching a cartoon and Alice dug out her blue glass spray bottle. Would Brian dare to lock up a thirteen-year-old? She tried to convince herself that he wouldn't. 'Please don't let me need this,' she said under her breath.

Sarah watched her wrap the bottle in a cloth and hide it in her bag. 'Do you think there will be a display of fruit on the banqueting table?' she asked.

*

By seven o'clock the girls were ready and waiting for Thomas in the lounge. Alice's parents had already taken lots of photographs of them, keen to record the unusual occasion of their daughter looking elegant. Her mum was feeling rather envious.

'Couldn't you have got a ticket for your dad and I?' she asked with mock indignation.

'Er, no, sorry. No fossils allowed.'

'You've got some nerve! We're younger than Lucinda's parents!'

Alice grinned.

'Her usual, complimentary self,' commented Thomas as he walked in.

'I have to say, Thomas, your friend who made these outfits is very talented,' said his mother.

'She certainly is. She's managed to make Alice look like a girl.'

They all laughed as Thomas ducked to miss a cushion that was thrown across the room.

'Alright, you both look very nice,' he admitted. 'Though I'm disappointed you're not wearing the rabbit slippers you had on this morning.'

'They're upstairs if you want to borrow them while we're out,' said Alice.

'I might take you up on that. Come on. You shall go to the ball!' He picked up their bags and carried them out to the car. 'There's some weight in these, are you worried you won't like the food?'

'Shh! You know very well what's in there.'

'Well, you couldn't ask for more festive scenery, could you?' said their father, shivering as he stepped out of the front door. The frosted landscape already had a blanket of snow and a few more flakes were trying their best to top it up.

'Oh no … we're not going in the Mini are we?' asked Alice in dismay.

'I'm sorry, did m'lady order a carriage? You know I'm not insured to drive Dad's car!'

Alice pulled a face.

'He only needs to drop us at the end of the main drive, doesn't he?' Sarah reminded her.

She pulled the passenger seat forward and squeezed into the back, taking care to pull her dress and cloak in around her. Alice sat in the front and waved goodbye to her parents before putting her mask on.

'At least no one will know it's me. Fancy going to the ball in a Mini!'

'You've turned into a dreadful snob, considering you didn't even have an invitation this time last week!' said Thomas.

'We do have a chauffeur, though,' Sarah pointed out.

'Thank you. And how many chauffeurs would come back in a couple of hours to wait in a rowing boat in the freezing cold?'

'Well, that depends on how many guests would abandon a party to search for some old bloke they've never met,' retorted Alice.

'Touché,' sighed Thomas in his usual manner.

On arrival at the castle they saw a knight on horseback outside the gate house and a gazebo with a green and gold flag on the top. Guests were sheltering from a light flurry of snow as they waited for the next carriage to transport them up to the castle. The entrance and driveway were lit by burning torches.

'Not as good as the ones in the village, are they?' Thomas remarked. 'These torches are guzzling oil.'

'Spot the geek!' muttered Alice, as she got out of the car and helped her friend out of the back seat.

'See you later! Behave yourselves!' Thomas waved as he drove off.

Hiding their oversized evening bags beneath their cloaks, the girls made sure their masks were in place and joined the group huddled under the gazebo.

'Wow!' exclaimed a tall American lady with flame-red hair. 'You two look fabulous. I think I went to the wrong hire shop! I'm Amber, by the way and this is my partner, Zack.'

'Nice to meet you,' they replied and introduced themselves.

A giant court jester, or rather a man on stilts juggling burning torches, appeared from behind some trees, making Sarah jump.

'My lords and ladies, the next carriage is approaching,' he announced. He caught all three torches and took a bow as a resplendent gold carriage drawn by two black horses ground to a halt. A footman jumped down and opened the door.

'Room for four more.'

Another carriage arrived as that one departed. The girls took the third one, sharing it with Amber and Zack. They looked around in fascination as the carriage rumbled up the cobblestone drive to the imposing castle building.

'Moving, isn't it?' said Amber, noticing Alice's eyes welling up.

'Er … yes. Gets me every time,' fibbed Alice, taking out a handkerchief. It was actually Amber's overpowering perfume making her eyes water.

When they pulled up outside the entrance hall the footman helped them out of the carriage. They were greeted on the steps by a 'lord' in exquisite medieval costume, wearing a long curly wig and a black mask. He shook hands with fellow lords, asking if they had encountered any highwaymen on their journey, and kissed ladies on the hand. He held Alice's hand a little too long for her liking. Creepy. Thankfully, she was wearing gloves, but she still wiped the back of her hand on her cloak as they were led inside to meet their hosts.

In the entrance hall, where the air was heady with the aroma of mulled wine, stood the biggest Christmas tree the girls had ever seen, decorated in gold and red. They had to stand in front of it for the photographer, who insisted on snapping all guests as they arrived. There were people dressed as monks, knights, kings, queens, jesters and even one as Robin Hood. An enormous chandelier adorned with holly had a large bunch of mistletoe suspended from the centre. Fire-breathers wearing menacing eye masks were positioned in each corner. True to their reputation, their hosts did not disappoint. Mr and Mrs Rowbottom, Isabella and Lucinda were waiting in the Red Room to welcome their guests. The girls tried to take in as much of the decor as they could, from the luxurious, though garish, red panelled walls, to an extravagant golden clock above the fireplace. Lucinda, looking like a pale porcelain doll in her beautiful red dress and black cape, appeared rather bored until she recognised Alice and Sarah.

'Oh, I'm so glad you made it!' she beamed. 'I was worried when I saw more snow that it might put people off. Your dresses are absolutely amazing!'

'Hello girls, lovely to see you,' said Mrs Rowbottom. 'Brian, these are Lucinda's friends from school, Alice and Sarah.'

Alice could feel herself trembling as Brian Rowbottom shook hands. She had almost expected an electric shock when their hands touched, but his expression didn't change. He was a giant of a man, who had more hair in his huge black moustache than on his head. There was something else strange about him; his dark green eyes seemed too small for the size of his face.

'Pleased to meet you,' he said in his booming voice. 'Lucinda speaks highly of you both.'

Alice doubted that were true.

'Help yourselves to a drink,' he insisted. 'The red and green cocktails are the non-alcoholic ones. Wench!' he called, clicking his fingers at a waitress in medieval attire.

She brought over a tray of the mysterious striped drinks in champagne flutes.

'Incredible!' exclaimed Sarah, taking a sip. 'Strawberry … and then melon, in alternate layers!'

Alice wondered if it was a special Sinwip cocktail.

'Follow me,' said Lucinda, 'I want to show you the surprise entertainment.'

They followed her to the far window.

'There it is!' she announced proudly. 'Our very own Christmas funfair.'

The girls couldn't believe their eyes. The courtyard had been transformed into a large-scale fairground with dazzling lights and dizzy music. They could see a merry-go-round, bumper cars, even a full-size big wheel, while more jesters on stilts were wandering around with candy floss and toffee apples. Alice spotted Father Christmas leaning against a Hook-a-Duck stall eating a candy cane.

'He shouldn't be doing that,' observed Lucinda, frowning. 'Mind you, now it's really snowing, he doesn't need to operate the snow machine. We got one just in case, you see.'

No, Alice didn't see. How was it possible to worry about laying on fake snow when there was an old man imprisoned here somewhere? She forced a smile. Sarah didn't need to. She had that gormless grin on her face again.

'It's just unbelievable,' said Alice, truthfully.

'I just can't believe I'm here!' admitted Sarah.

'Enjoy the evening,' said Lucinda. 'You'll find more drinks and some canapés in the next room. I'll meet up with you later.'

The girls wandered into the adjoining Cedar Room, which was similar to the previous, but with even more sinister portraits looking down at them from elaborate gilt frames. Alice was amused to see waxwork figures of ladies playing the harp and flute to entertain a waxwork Earl of Aylesford and his guests. As they made their way towards the table around which real guests were gathering, Alice stopped dead. She had spotted the centrepiece, an incredible ice sculpture. But Alice had not paused to admire the skill of the artist – she was rooted to the spot in horror because she was gazing at a sculpture of herself.

'Come on, what's up?' asked Sarah, turning to pull on her arm. 'Why have you ... oh my life! It's you!' she said as she caught sight of the ice sculpture towering above them. It certainly appeared to be Alice. Her face, her oversized wings, her hair ...

'Brian must know ...' whispered Alice, panic-stricken. She started to feel sick with fear.

Eventually, Sarah snorted with laughter and slapped Alice on the back.

'What a pair of idiots!' she chuckled. 'It's not you at all, it's meant to be an angel.'

'What? Are you sure?' asked Alice.

'Look to the side. Can you see the halo at the back of her head?'

'Oh, yes. Blimey, my heart's racing, I really thought we'd been rumbled.'

'Alice Parker with a halo? We can laugh that one off!' Sarah delved into her bag for her camera.

Alice was red with embarrassment.

'Look, if it makes you feel better, I thought the same at first. And you are a frosty cow at times!'

Alice wanted to hit Sarah with her bag, but knew that the weight of its contents might do some damage. She smiled sheepishly.

'Ooh, wait for it!' said Sarah as she reached the table. 'Frosty has even got a giant bowl of fruit in front of her! It is you after all!' She passed Alice some red grapes.

'Very funny.'

They browsed trays of cocktails, watched a waitress pouring a champagne fountain and helped themselves to small gold cups passed around on trays by waiters. These contained tasters of traditional medieval dishes. Although they were unusual, the girls liked them. Katy and Olivia were nearby, but promptly turned away when they made eye contact. Mingling was out of the question, since they didn't know anyone else here.

Alice looked around feeling rather awkward and her gaze rested on a haunting figure across the room. Standing next to the fireplace was a man dressed as a plague doctor. His grim white mask with glass eyes had a long beak that protruded from his wide-brimmed leather hat. She remembered from a history lesson that those beak doctors signified that death was imminent, and couldn't help wondering if it was a sign. The black cloak looked particularly sinister compared with the colourful outfits around him. He nodded at Alice and touched his hat with his cane. She took a step back and reached out for her friend. Sarah had her back to him, staring at a painting.

'Oi!' hissed Alice. When she turned to point out the morbid character, he had disappeared. 'Oh! He's gone! Never mind …' She shuddered and pulled her cloak around her, chilled by the sensation of cold water trickling down her spine. Who was he?

Admiring the furniture and over-the-top artefacts passed the remaining time during pre-dinner drinks, until they were summoned to the Great Hall for the banquet. Everyone moved slowly and politely, which was impressive, considering there must have been a hundred and fifty guests or more.

The Great Hall was just as Alice remembered it from childhood visits, with its chequered floor and immense sideboard, hand-carved from a single tree. Like the rest of the castle, the room smelled of old wood, worn leather and spices. Usually it was cordoned off by thick rope barriers, and she looked up at the balconies where tourists could stand and take photographs during the day. There was another magnificent Christmas tree in one corner and miniature Christmas trees on the tables, along with cascading arrangements of holly, poinsettias and candles. Suits of armour were residing in alcoves, one of which had no head and gave Sarah the creeps. Swords and shields were displayed on the walls and large antlers above every door. In one corner, a stuffed black bear was standing as if ready to fight. At the opposite end of the room to the Christmas tree was an artificial horse with a knight on its back, monitoring proceedings.

The girls were directed to their seats at one of three long tables, which ran almost the length of the room. Alice searched anxiously for the plague doctor but couldn't see him.

'Do you feel like we're being watched as well?' asked Sarah, looking over her shoulder.

'Yes. Who do you think it is?'

'The knight on the horse. And the bear. They're spooking me!'

Alice smiled. Perhaps the plague doctor wouldn't be at the banquet. He wouldn't be able to eat wearing that mask, anyway.

Jugs of wine and fruit juice were plentiful and the food never-ending, while they were entertained by singers, dancers and acrobats. Course after course was served – some the girls enjoyed, some they didn't. By the end their stomachs felt ready to explode. Alice had appreciated the variety of fruit and vegetables combined with meat, but was worried that she wouldn't be able to run up the stairs in the tower. Still, if she *was* captured by Brian, she wouldn't feel hungry for a long time. She looked at her watch. It was just before 10 o'clock. She nudged Sarah.

'When on earth will we be able to sneak off?' she whispered.

'Soon,' she replied. 'Looks like we're moving into the ballroom now.'

She was right. Brian Rowbottom was at the end of the room, trying in vain to get the attention of his merry and very noisy guests. He banged a metal jug on the table.

'Lords and ladies, may I have your attention for a moment? I hope you have all enjoyed the fine banquet and entertainment. My wife and I would be glad if you would accompany us in the ballroom at 10 o'clock. After the first dance, the funfair will also be open.' He paused for the applause, drunken hoots, whistles and banging of cups on the table.

'You may also have noticed a wax seal next to your plate, which is holding a green ribbon in place. If you care to break the seal and pull this ribbon, you should find a small Christmas gift from our family. Merry Christmas to you all!'

There was more clapping before the guests began pulling ribbons. As the girls tugged on theirs, two small parcels fell on to the table with a thud, appearing from within the floral arrangement nearest to them. Alice opened hers to find a beautiful silver necklace with a horse pendant. Sarah's was also a necklace, but with a silver shoe instead of a horse.

'Wow!' declared Sarah. 'What a generous, thoughtful present.'

'Lucinda must have chosen these,' said Alice. 'Look at mine.' She showed Sarah the horse. 'I feel awful now.'

'Now isn't the time,' Sarah insisted. 'We'll have one dance, then go. That funfair is a stroke of luck, no one will notice what we're doing, they'll be too busy enjoying themselves.'

In the ballroom, they found Lucinda and thanked her for the gifts. She introduced them to two of her cousins, Oliver and Damian, so that they had a partner for the dance. As Lucinda dashed off, the four of them felt rather awkward.

'Can you dance?' Alice asked Damian.

'Enough to get by at these awful events,' he grinned. 'Can you?'

'No. I'm afraid I'm going to look an idiot.'

Sarah was quite happy dancing, and as the music began and the Rowbottoms took the floor, she and Oliver were among the first couples to join them. Alice followed grudgingly, led by Damian, and felt very much out of her depth. She looked across at Sarah and Oliver.

'Don't they make you sick!' she said to Damian.

'All these stuck-up toffs? Always!' he laughed. Alice laughed too, though that wasn't what she had meant. Suddenly she spied the plague doctor again, who seemed to be staring at her from a distance.

'Who *is* that?' she asked nervously. 'Why would anyone choose to wear something as horrible as that?'

Damian grinned. 'That's our cousin, Hugh,' he replied. 'He's always been a bit weird.'

Alice was slightly relieved. When the dance ended, she felt reluctant to make her excuses. The boys were funny and she had enjoyed their company – it was hard to believe they were related to Brian.

'Perhaps we'll see you at the fair!' said Oliver.

'Perhaps!' replied Sarah, putting her bag over her shoulder. 'We just need to look for a friend first.'

Alice was pulled by Sarah towards a group of people so that they could disappear into a crowd. Then they made their way around the outside of the ballroom to the doors leading outside. The dancing continued, but they could see Oliver and Damian sitting down looking fed up.

For a few minutes they wandered around the fair, trying to blend in. They had a ride on the big wheel so that Alice could study the South Tower. She was hoping to spot a glimmer of light in one of the windows, but it was in complete darkness.

Back on the ground, Alice suggested that Sarah should have a go at Hook-a-Duck, the nearest stall to the tower, so that she could keep the door in sight. She needed her route to the tower to be clear, but there were a few people milling around nearby.

'Oh no!' shrieked Sarah. 'I've caught a frog instead of a duck!'

Alice rolled her eyes. The guests near the tower began to make their way towards them to see what the fuss was about. Her path was clear! 'Well done, Sarah!' she muttered. She wasn't congratulating her on winning a family pass to the castle, though.

The people observing clapped politely, giving Alice the jitters. They reminded her of macabre puppets in their masks.

By now she had the key ready and a torch in her left hand, hidden under her cloak. 'I'll go first,' she whispered to Sarah. 'Wait here, then follow me when you see I'm in.' She pulled up her hood and slipped away, keeping to the shadows against the wall of the castle. The windows were much higher up than she had imagined, way above her head; that ruled out one escape route. If she tried to jump from one of those, she'd probably break her ankle.

The lock was rusty. Alice had to fiddle with the key for what seemed like an age until the door opened.

Soon she was joined by Sarah.

'Anyone follow us?' she asked, appearing from behind the door.

'No. Ooh, it stinks in here, all fusty and spooky.'

'It smells burnt, that's all,' whispered Alice. 'Have your torch ready in case this one dies.'

She rushed up the spiral stone steps to the first floor, Sarah running after her. There were four doors. The first door opened when she turned the handle. When she called out, the only reply was an echo. She did the same at the next door, and the next. Nothing.

'On to the next floor.'

They carried on up the stairs, Sarah letting out a scream as she ran through a cobweb.

'Shhh! I know. I don't like it either. I'm glad you came with me,' admitted Alice.

Four more doors. This time Sarah opened them. They waited and listened. Suddenly they heard a scratching sound.

'Theo?' called Alice.

Sarah drew a sharp breath and grabbed Alice's arm as something ran over her feet. Alice shone the torch at the floor to see a rat scampering down the steps.

'I take it that wasn't him,' said Sarah, trying to make a joke of it, although she was shaking like a leaf.

The twelfth door was locked. Shining her torch on the bunch of keys, Alice searched frantically for one labelled '3 – 4.' When Sarah opened the door, Alice pushed past her and stepped in to an elegant room with a four-poster bed and tapestries covering the walls. There was no sign of life other than the disapproving faces of bearded men, who were frowning upon her from their paintings. She called Theo but there was no response.

Alice was clearly panicking. 'He's not here, is he?' she ranted, storming out of the room and slamming the door behind her. 'He flippin' well isn't here, Grandad got it wrong.'

She banged on the door with her fists and sank to the floor in tears. 'I've blown it,' she sobbed. 'I can't find him and I don't know where else to look.'

'We've done our best,' insisted Sarah. She shone her torch up the steps and peered up to the fourth floor. 'There aren't any doors up there, it's been destroyed by fire. It's just one big, stone room.'

Alice let out a moan.

'Pull yourself together,' ordered Sarah. 'We could do without your wings making an appearance.'

Alice nodded and lifted her mask to wipe her face. Then she froze. 'Did you hear that?'

'What?'

Alice turned around and put her ear to the door she had been leaning against. She could hear a dull thudding sound. She knocked three times. There was a pause, then three muffled knocks could just be made out coming from inside.

'That must be him!'

She flung the door open and dashed back into the room. 'Theo?' called Alice cautiously.

'If that skanky rat appears again, I won't be ...' Sarah's protest was interrupted by knocking. It was coming from the panelled wall at the far side of the room. A hidden room? The girls thumped all the panels with the palm of their hand, desperately trying to find a way of opening up the wall. Eventually Alice stood up, breathless, and looked around again. 'You can wipe that smug look off your face!' she snapped at the small oil painting above them, before lashing out at it with her torch. Click. Then came a grating sound as the partition wall slid open just wide enough for a person to squeeze through. The girls peered inside.

An elderly man was lying on the floor at their feet, where he must have fallen in his efforts to make himself heard. Alice stepped over him to get in to the room and crouched down beside him.

'You must be Theo,' she said, squeezing his hand. 'I'm John Parker's granddaughter.' He smiled and closed his eyes. 'We've come to get you. Don't give up now!' she begged him. 'Are you hurt? Can we sit you up?'

Theo looked at her and nodded feebly. They lifted him carefully into a sitting position so that his back rested against a cupboard, though he couldn't help but let out a shout. He was clearly suffering, but he raised his hand to signal he was alright. Realising that this tiny room had no windows, so no one would see their torches, Alice positioned both of them on top of the cupboard so they could see what they were doing.

'Thank you,' mumbled Theo. He looked pale and weak, his hair was matted and his clothes dirty. Alice wasn't sure if he'd always had a beard or if this one had grown in the last six weeks. She showed him the fruit and pineapple juice that they had brought with them. 'Would you like these?' she asked. 'We need you to be strong enough to walk out of here with us.'

'There's a party going on outside,' added Sarah. 'Don't worry, we've brought you a costume.' She handed it over before wandering back out to the landing.

Theo perked up at the sight of the fruit. He took the banana and fumbled with it, trying to peel it. Alice helped him. He savoured the first mouthful as if he had never tasted one before. Then he wolfed down the rest and reached for the grapes, followed by the pineapple juice. Leaning his head back, he let out a long sigh of relief.

'I've hardly had any fruit since I've been here,' he said quietly. 'They've kept me as weak as possible, apart from when they needed me.'

'That's exactly what Imogen predicted. Now, I'm afraid we've got to hurry, the others are waiting for us. Here's your costume.' When she pulled it out of Sarah's bag, they realised it was a jester's outfit, comprising a tunic, hat, and tights with one red leg and one yellow.

'Oh, no!' moaned Theo. 'Haven't I been punished enough already? Is this Imogen's idea of a joke?'

Alice laughed. 'Well, you'll certainly blend in, there are a few jesters here tonight. Let us know if you need some help,' she said, stepping out of the room to let him get changed.

She crashed into Sarah, who was rushing back through the main bedroom.

'I thought I heard a noise,' she whispered. They both peered out of the bottom corner of the window.

'Oh my life, I did! Someone just left the tower, look!'

A lone, hooded figure was quickening his pace away from the tower towards the funfair.

'Well, I doubt he knew *we* were in here,' said Alice, flustered.

'He must have guessed *someone* was in here. Let's just go,' pleaded Sarah anxiously.

Alice stared after the figure in the shadows. Suddenly, he stopped in his tracks and turned to look back at the tower. Alice gasped – she could recognise that profile even in the darkness. That long white beak was unmistakable.

Theo emerged from his room pulling on his three-point jester's hat and mask. The girls couldn't even raise a smile.

'Someone's onto us,' blurted out Sarah.

'It's Brian's nephew, Hugh,' said Alice.

Theo suddenly looked afraid. 'We need to move. NOW!'

They closed the secret panel. Alice locked the outer door behind them and they began the awkward descent, trying to help the frail old man down the narrow spiral steps. Alice went first, supporting him by the arm, while Sarah followed gripping the back of his tunic in case he fell. With every step, the bells on Theo's hat jingled merrily.

Alice sniffed the air. 'Can you smell something?' she whispered.

'It's probably me. I haven't had a bath in weeks,' replied Theo.

'No, not that, a burning smell.'

'It stinks of fire damage upstairs,' said Sarah.

Mysteriously, the smell became stronger as they descended, then as the staircase twisted down to the first floor, they were suddenly met by smoke. Further down they could make out a bright flickering light.

'Turn back,' croaked Theo, 'it's been torched again!'

They managed to turn on the steps and headed back up.

'What next?' screeched Sarah, terrified. 'Fourth floor upwards is burnt out!'

Alice didn't answer, paralysed by fear.

'The stone steps are still OK,' said Theo. 'We need to get on to the roof, it's the only option. The door leading back into the main building is on the ground floor as well.'

They scrambled up the steps as fast as they could. Perhaps it was the adrenaline giving Theo a boost, but this time around, in spite of being in pain himself, he was dragging Alice who was struggling. He was right, the steps were fine and they left the charred upper floors behind them to reach the seventh floor. Here, they found a wrought-iron ladder leading to a trapdoor in the ceiling.

Alice had to let Sarah climb up first and push it open; she felt too weak. When she lifted her head, she saw Sarah shining the torch down the ladder. She could barely find the rungs with her feet, and Theo helped her up. Sarah grabbed her arm, and as soon as Alice was out on the flat roof, she flopped down on the snow-covered asphalt.

'Alice, are you alright? Did you inhale too much smoke?' asked Sarah, with fear in her voice. Alice stretched out her arm towards her bag but it was too late. Sarah spotted some movement in Alice's cloak and knew what was coming. 'NO! Not now, PLEASE!'

'Sorry,' groaned Alice, getting into a kneeling position. She pulled her cloak to one side and remembered to her relief that Freya had designed her dress with a low back. Just as well. Within seconds, her immense wings were quivering in the icy breeze, as high as the turrets around them.

'Oh ... dear ...' said Theo gravely. 'Were you hoping to fly out of here? *I* can't, my wings are too small.'

Alice shook her head.

'No, that wasn't the plan,' replied Sarah, sitting down next to him. 'They're waiting for us in rowing boats down there.'

When Alice eventually got to her feet, she peered out from behind a turret to look down at the river. They were so high up, it was impossible to make out anything on the water apart from the reflection of the moon. Smoke was beginning to pour out of the tower now, and a fire engine's siren could be heard in the distance. She took out her mobile, then threw it down in temper. No signal. 'Is your phone working, Sarah?' she asked.

Sarah pulled a face and showed her the screen. '*Network not available*'.

'We could try signalling to them with a torch,' suggested Theo. 'Do you know Morse Code?'

'No,' Alice replied. But she rested her torch between two turrets and began to flash it on and off. She paused and looked down at the river. Still nothing but darkness and smoke. 'I should spray my wings,' she decided. 'If we've no option but to wait for the fire brigade, I need to get rid of them.'

'Don't be too hasty,' said Theo. 'At least you've got a second chance of escape. I can't see us being rescued from up here.'

'Don't say that,' pleaded Alice. 'This is all my fault. If I hadn't agreed to find you, you would still be safe in that room.'

'Believe me, I'd rather be up here. I'm very grateful to you.'

Alice got up and walked to the other side of the roof, shivering. She looked down into the courtyard. She could see that the guests had been ushered away from the fair and back towards the ballroom, where a crowd had gathered to see the tower on fire. Surely they'd had enough entertainment for one evening? She shone a light at her feet so that she didn't trip over one of the many objects cluttering the roof.

'What's all this?' she wondered. 'Fireworks?' She followed an array of wires along an enormous quantity of rockets until she came to a digital timer that read '7.46.' It was counting down by the second.

'No!' She looked at her watch. 10.52pm. 'There's a whole display of fireworks over here, due to go off at 11 o'clock! We need to move!'

Theo got up to examine it. 'I daren't risk meddling with that. And we can rule out going back in there,' he said, nodding towards the trapdoor. 'There's too much smoke already. All we can do is sit facing the wall on the far side.'

Sarah covered her face with her hands. Alice went to join her. She could see tears running down Sarah's cheeks in the torchlight and put her arm around her.

'If only my grandson could see me now,' sighed Theo. 'An escaped prisoner sitting on the roof of a castle in a jester's outfit, waiting for a firework display. He'd find it funny.'

'Sounds like a weirdo,' muttered Alice.

'You're right there!' he chuckled. They sat in silence for a moment. The sound of breaking glass told them that the heat from the fire was smashing more windows.

Sarah wiped her eyes. 'I wonder which it will be,' she said, full of melancholy. 'Fire, fireworks or hypothermia that will finish us off.'

A smile crept across Theo's face. 'None of those!' he said, getting up on his feet and pointing to the sky behind the girls. They turned around to see where he was pointing. Something large and white was flying towards them through the smoke.

'What *on earth* is that?' wailed Sarah.

'It's Guinevere!' shrieked Alice, clapping her hands. 'Unbelievable! I didn't know unicorns could fly!'

'They can't. Unless they're Finwip unicorns,' explained Theo. 'Their wings only emerge if they sense strong emotions in the people they're close to.'

'Dad!' Guinevere's rider called out.

'It's Anna!' shouted Theo. 'You can land here love, but only briefly.'

'Four minutes until these fireworks go off!' Alice informed her, as Guinevere swooped down onto the roof.

'Take the girls first,' Theo ordered.

'No,' insisted Alice. 'I've got a second option, you said that yourself.'

'You've never tried flying!' cried Sarah.

'Now might be a good time.'

Anna pulled Sarah up onto Guinevere's back. Her father followed.

'You're a brave girl, Alice,' Theo told her. 'Thank you.'

They took off and Alice watched nervously as her friends were delivered safely to the river bank. She saw a tiny light moving towards them and guessed it must be someone from the boats running to meet them.

When Guinevere soared back up to the top of the tower, Alice was waiting, leaning over the wall. 'No time to land!' she called to Anna over the sound of beating wings, 'only seconds left before the fireworks start.'

Guinevere hovered as close as she could. 'Jump!' screamed Anna. As Alice balanced on the wall, her heart in her mouth, the first fireworks went off, wailing as their golden tails darted through the snow-filled sky. She jumped.

Amazingly, she landed on Guinevere's back, but her velvet gown slipped on her glossy coat and she hurtled backwards. She managed to grab her long tail and began to flap her wings in an attempt to counterbalance her weight. Terrified, she flapped her wings as fast as she could. Anna turned and stretched out her arm, but couldn't reach her.

'I'm OK,' Alice shouted. Indeed she was. She was actually flying, but daren't let go of Guinevere's tail. She could have burst with happiness. Her enormous wings were more than adequate to keep her airborne. Unfortunately, her landing wasn't as graceful. She had to break free as they neared the ground and in spite of flapping her wings, she landed with a thud in a clump of reeds.

'Alice!' yelled Thomas, running towards her. 'I was worried sick!'

She was half dragged, half carried to the remaining boat and Ethan started rowing as soon as they were seated. Alice sprayed her wings using the blue bottle – there was no way she'd fit in the van with those. As their boat moved away, she watched Anna spray Guinevere's, and once they had retracted, she galloped down the bank alongside them.

When they reached the car park, Ethan hid his boat with the first one, beneath some bushes on the river bank. Alice was amused to see Imogen waiting for them in a large Coffee Cauldron van driven by Fay. Along with Thomas and Ethan, she clambered into the back where she was reunited with Sarah, Theo, Grandad and Jake. Amidst laughter and congratulations, Alice waved goodbye to Anna and promised to meet her back at the village. Only when Thomas slammed the doors behind them did she breathe a sigh of relief.

As the van sped off, Anna had to laugh when she read the slogan on the back of it. *'The Coffee Cauldron – magical brews, magical experiences.'*

Chapter 13

Surprises and Suspicions

'Let the dust settle,' Grandad had advised her late on Saturday night. 'Things will sort themselves out.'

She certainly hoped so. After Sarah went home on Sunday morning, Alice hadn't mentioned the events of the party to anyone, apart from her parents, who had to be told about the fire as an excuse for being so late home. They saw it in the local paper on Monday morning anyway. Alice had been worrying about Hugh Rowbottom. What if he knew it was her and Sarah who were in the tower? Then there was the CCTV. Even wearing their masks, they might still be recognised by Lucinda. Thomas told her not to be so silly. Whatever Brian Rowbottom or his nephew knew, they wouldn't let on. They couldn't admit to kidnapping Theo and holding him captive, could they? Furthermore, Brian should be smart enough to realise that if he compromised Finwip society any more, his own secret identity would be at risk.

Even though she couldn't erase that hideous beak mask from her mind, Alice turned her attention to the celebrations planned in the village this evening. She wasn't sure she could face another party so soon, but didn't want to miss it either.

'Another one?' her mother had queried. 'You're popular, all of a sudden!'

'Perhaps her friends have realised what a good-looking brother she's got. I'm going as well,' said Thomas.

'Where's this one being held?' their mother asked.

'Oh, just down the road,' explained Thomas. 'We won't be late this time, it starts at 6 o'clock.'

'As long as you're at home tomorrow night,' she said. 'You know I like us all to have dinner together on Christmas Eve.'

*

Soon after Sarah had arrived for the village party, the Parkers' doorbell rang again.

'Alice, you've got a visitor,' shouted Thomas.

She rushed down the stairs, but hesitated when she saw who was standing in the hall.

'Lucinda!' she exclaimed, trying to sound pleased. 'Sarah, Lucinda's here,' she called, hoping for back-up to ease her awkwardness.

'Oh, I'm sorry if you're busy,' Lucinda began. 'Only, I wanted to apologise for the chaos at the end of the night on Saturday. I didn't see you again and I wanted to make sure you were OK.'

'We were absolutely fine, thank you,' said Sarah with a reassuring smile as she joined them. 'Actually, we slipped away early. Alice wasn't feeling well again, so we had to dash after the first dance.'

Alice nodded, relieved at Sarah's swift response.

'Oh, that explains it,' said Lucinda. 'Oliver and Damian were looking for you as well. I think they liked you!'

'Er, well, they seemed nice,' said Alice, blushing.

'Mind you,' said Lucinda, suddenly looking glum, 'I'm not sure I'd get involved with a Rowbottom. My dad has been in the most awful mood since the party. And it can't be because of the fire. That tower wasn't used anyway.'

Alice and Sarah exchanged worried glances.

'Perhaps he feels the fire ruined the evening,' suggested Alice.

'Maybe. But there's something else.' She wiped away a tear with a pink tissue. 'Listen, don't tell anyone, will you? But I heard him on the phone and he said he might lose the castle because his 'financial circumstances' have changed. Whatever that means. Do you think we'll lose our house?' she asked, blowing her nose loudly.

'Oh, I'm so sorry!' blurted out Alice.

'We're both sorry to hear that,' said Sarah, frowning at Alice. 'But I'm sure it won't come to that, whatever happens. Your dad is a very clever and successful man, isn't he?'

Lucinda nodded.

'Would you like to sit down and have a drink?' asked Alice, feeling silly after her initial reaction.

'No, thanks. I should go, my mum's waiting in the car. I brought this with me, it's very good.'

She handed Alice a large brown envelope. She pulled out the photograph of her and Sarah in front of the Christmas tree at the ball.

'That is good!' said Alice with a grin. 'Thank you. We'll never forget the party, I promise you.'

'I'm glad,' sniffed Lucinda. 'Bye then.'

'I hope you still have a good Christmas,' said Alice quietly as she opened the door. The girls waved as Lucinda walked down the path.

Once she had gone, Alice sank down on the bottom stair, looking at the photograph.

'How bad do I feel now?' she moaned.

'Not half as bad as you look,' said Thomas, putting on his coat. 'Come on, we'll be late.'

Sarah helped Alice to her feet.

'Poor Lucinda,' Alice said softly on the way to the oak tree. 'It's not her fault, poor thing.'

'Blimey! Are you feeling alright? You're not trying to be nice are you?' Thomas asked. 'Please don't worry about it tonight. It will be all right, I'm sure. I hate to say it, but Brian always lands on his feet.'

*

Down in the village they went straight to the changing rooms to put on their Finwip robes.

'I'm desperate to let my wings out. They could do with a stretch!' said Thomas.

'Hold on,' ordered Alice, 'I still don't know how to make my wings come out. Imogen wouldn't let me have one of those red bottles.'

'I'm not surprised! That's potent stuff. Mmm, it's not easy to explain, but I'll have a go. You know how our wings respond to negative emotions, when you're angry or afraid? Well, they respond to positive ones in the same way. You need to concentrate on how much you want them to appear. Relax, clear your mind, then try to focus on something that makes you really happy.'

Alice pulled a face.

'I'll save you some food, you'll probably miss the buffet,' said Sarah. Thomas sniggered.

'I don't know why I put up with you two,' declared Alice, trying to hide her smile as she entered the changing rooms.

When she found her dress and closed the curtain behind her, she stared at her reflection in the mirror. She was ashamed to admit to herself that Sarah was right. This could take a while. What did make her really happy these days? She sat down on an old wooden stool and racked her brain. Oh dear. Maybe … maybe the happiest she had felt for a while was on Saturday night, when she was flying. It had only been for a few seconds, but it was wonderful. It felt so normal, if that were possible. Like a natural progression in her life. Landing needed some practice, though.

She changed into her robes, brushed her hair and then sat back down on the stool. She took a deep breath and closed her eyes. Concentrating on that brief experience of flying, she tried to remember exactly how she had felt. It had been both terrifying and exhilarating. The fear of falling was pushed aside by the realisation that this was who she really was. A Finwip who could fly. A thirteen year-old who had the potential to achieve anything, if she put her mind to it. Of course, this had always been true – Alice just hadn't been aware of it. She smiled to herself at the thought of those oversized wings carrying her down from the tower and soon began to feel movement under the skin on her back. It was working!

'That's it! Come on!' she encouraged them, as if they could hear her.

'Alice? Are you alright in there?' Sarah banged on the partition wall then went out and opened the curtain of Alice's cubicle. Thwack. She staggered backwards having been smacked across the face by the tip of a very large wing.

'Oh! I'm so sorry,' said Alice, trying not to laugh.

'It's alright. I see you managed it, then. Well done you,' Sarah congratulated her, rubbing her stinging left cheek.

Alice was very pleased with herself. That had been easier than she thought, and the dress performed brilliantly again, allowing her wings to emerge through the purposely-designed gaps.

Sarah, now that she had her own robes, looked like the cat that got the cream.

'Your purple cloak really suits you,' remarked Alice. 'Even without wings. A pointed hat would just finish it off, though. And a broomstick.'

'Cheeky cow. I love it!' beamed Sarah. 'Come on, I'm starving.'

They hurried along the corridor, admiring bunches of berry-laden holly and clusters of golden bells which were hanging beneath the torches. They could hear music and laughter coming from the dining hall and when they pushed the door open, what a sight they were met with.

Hovering around tables piled high with superb dishes were more wings and pointed ears than the girls had seen before. It was like stepping into a scene from a fairytale, as fifty or so Finwips dressed in a rainbow of colours laughed and joked whilst tucking in to a veritable feast. The fire was burning beneath the huge central cauldron, from which Fay was ladling mulled apple juice into mugs. There was one curved table for savoury dishes and one for sweet. Sarah had seen a chocolate fountain before, but not a butterscotch fountain. Next to it were fruit kebabs displayed in half a giant watermelon, looking like a porcupine that had rolled in fruit. There were raspberry and redcurrant jellies, and green mint mousse in goblets with a candy cane hooked on the side. There were normal things, like Christmas pudding, mince pies and brandy sauce, but also a tower of chocolate profiteroles filled with banana cream. A striking blue spruce Christmas tree was smothered in edible decorations – strings of dried fruit, nuts, popcorn and fruit leather ribbons were winding around gingerbread shapes and sparkling sweets. Alice was overjoyed to find stained-glass window biscuits, which she hadn't seen since she was small.

'They're here!' Thomas shouted. Everyone put down their plates and cups and began to clap. There were whistles and cheers as Imogen, Theo and Anna came over to welcome them. The girls felt very embarrassed.

'I'm sure I speak for us all when I say we owe you a huge thank you,' said Imogen.

'More than we can put into words!' added Anna, giving her dad a hug. Theo nodded and smiled.

'This year's Christmas party is a special one,' Imogen continued. 'We are celebrating the safe return of Theo, we officially welcome you, Alice and Sarah, to our village and we thank you for what you have already done for us!'

More clapping and whistling followed. The girls looked at each other, feeling more awkward by the minute.

'To show our appreciation, we would like to present you with a gift. These gifts are usually reserved for those who have been a valued member of Finwip society for many years and who have shown dedication to preserving it.'

Alice saw Thomas helping their grandad to the front of the crowd with his camera and tripod.

'However,' said Imogen, 'you two have shown selflessness and generosity to your subterranean friends when you have known us for barely a fortnight. The aim of Finwip communities is to revive the age-old trait which used to distinguish us from our contemporaries above ground. That is superiority in vision and understanding. We feel that you have achieved this already, which is remarkable.'

'Hear, hear,' said Theo as he stepped forward with two small boxes. He took Alice's right arm and fastened a heavy silver bracelet around her wrist. A smooth and perfectly oval agate stone in the centre was flanked by intricately engraved wings. An identical bracelet was placed on Sarah's wrist. Next, Anna presented them with a bouquet of flowers each and some chocolates - from The Coffee Cauldron, of course. The girls were overwhelmed as everyone applauded again and the camera flashed.

'Oh no,' whispered Alice, squirming at being centre of attention. 'We didn't want all this.'

'Speak for yourself!' replied Sarah, posing for another photo.

When the noise died down and the crowd dispersed, Alice turned to Anna.

'We didn't do that much,' she said. 'You had to rescue us all, in the end.'

'It wouldn't have been possible without you,' Anna maintained. 'Anyway, it was Guinevere really. I can't fly. I will always be in your debt. If there's ever anything I can help you with, please let me know.' She gave the girls a hug.

'We will. Thank you,' said Alice.

The girls finally made their way to the food, hardly able to take their eyes off their bracelets.

'What an honour,' said Sarah. 'And I'm not even a Finwip!'

'You are now!' replied Alice, loading her plate with a selection of desserts. She hadn't even looked at the savouries. They joined Thomas and her grandparents, who were sitting in one of the alcoves. There were kisses and congratulations all round.

'We're so proud of you both,' said her grandma.

'Chip off the old block!' affirmed Grandad.

'Will you come and sit by me again?' Grandma asked Sarah. 'Their wings take up so much room in here!'

'Gladly!' she replied.

They were the last group to finish eating, by the time Grandma had insisted that they try each of the desserts she had made.

'Where is everyone?' asked Alice as she stood up from the table and looked outside the alcove.

'In the forest I expect,' said Thomas.

'Forest? Which forest? What for?'

'Oh, I forgot, you haven't been there yet, have you?' realised Thomas. 'Grandad, I think you should lead the way!'

Rubbing his hands, Grandad led the group into the kitchen and held open a door next to the larder.

'Step this way!' he insisted, pointing inside.

'Not another lift,' moaned Alice. 'Even if it is a large one.'

The five of them could squeeze in. Seconds later, Grandad opened the door and ushered Alice outside. They were, quite literally, outside. She stepped out from the trunk of an enormous pine to find herself in the clearing of a wood.

Sarah jumped up and down clapping her hands. 'It just gets better!' she laughed.

In the middle of the clearing towered an immense fir tree, glowing with coloured lights from top to bottom. Some Finwips were dancing round it, others were sitting on benches carved from logs, enjoying a drink around the fire. The trees on the edge of the clearing were dotted with glass lanterns made from coloured jars and bottles, and a group of musicians with pointed ears wandered around playing their guitar, violin and flute. There were cocoon-like wooden swings hanging from some of the trees, which one or two people could sit in.

They reminded Alice of giant conkers which had been hollowed out.

'Good enough?' Thomas asked his sister, prodding her in the ribs.

'It's … magical!' whispered Alice. 'Where exactly are we?'

'This wood belongs to the farm where the unicorns have their paddock. In fact, their stable is just beyond those trees,' he explained, pointing into the distance.

'I take it the farmer is one of us, then?'

'Of course! Now, go and explore. We've got an hour or so before Mum will throw a fit.'

'Enjoy yourselves!' ordered Grandma and Grandad.

The girls ran to one of the conker swings and climbed in on to the soft cushions. They lay back and looked out at the stars. There wasn't a cloud in the sky.

'Do you know, I keep having to pinch myself to check that all this is real?' Sarah admitted.

'Snap!' said Alice. 'I wouldn't change it now, though.'

'Don't you dare!'

They closed their eyes for a moment before there was a knock on the side of the conker. It was Theo.

'I hope you don't mind me disturbing you,' he began, 'only I'd like to introduce you to my grandson.'

'Good evening, ladies!' said a cheeky, familiar face that popped up in front of the swing.

'No way!'

'Seb? You can't be!'

'And why not?' asked Seb indignantly.

'You're not a Finwip! *Are* you?' demanded Alice.

'No. *I'm* not, but Mum and Grandad are. I told you my mum had the same symptoms as you but you obviously didn't believe me.'

'Anna is your mum?' asked Sarah in disbelief.

'Yep. She's not as brainy as you though, Alice. She can't help me with maths homework.'

'I can, if you like,' Alice offered. Seb nodded vigorously.

'I think you three have some catching up to do!' laughed Theo. 'I'll leave you to it.'

The girls jumped down from the swing and they all made their way to a bench near the fire. Seb fetched drinks for them.

'Well, here we are!' he grinned.

'I still don't get it,' protested Alice. 'Why haven't we seen you in the village before?'

'Mum became very protective when Grandad went missing. He was taken just as he arrived at the great oak, you see. She wouldn't let me near the village or the castle, she said she wasn't prepared to lose anyone else. Not that I'd be any use to the Rowbottom empire!'

'Well, I've never seen your mum outside school,' said Sarah, having thought about it.

'She's always working late. She has a cake-making business.'

'WOW! Really?' gasped Alice. 'I didn't know that!'

'Yes, they make cakes for special occasions. Ice sculptures too. In fact, you might have seen the one they made for the Rowbottoms' Christmas do.'

Alice's jaw dropped. Sarah nearly fell off the bench laughing.

'We certainly did!' she confirmed. 'It was so life-like!'

'Spitting image, I thought, when I saw it,' said Seb with a grin. 'Mum said she couldn't resist.'

Alice had to laugh.

Sarah noticed how happy she seemed this evening. Perhaps she had finally found her niche and realised how lucky she was.

Grandad came over to join them, looking over his shoulder before he sat down.

'I don't want your grandma eavesdropping,' he whispered. 'Anyway, you three, did you know that Brian Rowbottom has also bought Clifton Windmill?'

'No,' replied Alice. 'Why would he do that? There's nothing in it.'

'Exactly! It's just a derelict landmark. So tell me, why would anyone want it? I've been keeping an eye on it and there's been some activity there lately, with unmarked lorries unloading hundreds of crates.'

'Oh, enough already!' snapped Alice, putting her hands over her ears. 'I don't want to know.'

Sebastian leaned forward. 'That makes sense,' he said in a low voice. 'My mum's company has been commissioned to make a cake that's a replica of the windmill. They took the order last week.'

'When's it for?' asked Grandad.

'Not for a while. I think Mum said Easter.'

'Excellent, we've got plenty of time to suss things out,' said Grandad, relieved.

'*We*?' queried Alice, who had actually been listening all along.

'Please, can we just enjoy the Christmas holiday first?' begged Sarah. 'I've really been looking forward to it.'

'I think I'm starting to look forward to going back to school,' muttered Alice. Shocked at herself as she said those words aloud, she considered that to be the most remarkable transformation so far ...

My Other Titles

Alice Parker & The Mind Magician

Alice Parker & The Secret of Arcanum Cove

Alice Parker & The Sound of the Silent

One Strange Christmas

If you would like to be informed when new titles are published, please email nicolapalmerwriter@gmail.com

About the Author

Nicola Palmer lives in Warwickshire, England. She likes animals, chocolate, vegetables and coffee. One day she hopes to grow wings and live in an underground village.

Unfortunately, Nicola doesn't have a magic letterbox, but she can be contacted at:

facebook.com/AliceParkersAdventures
twitter.com/nicolalpalmer
nicolapalmerwriter.blogspot.com

If you have enjoyed reading this book, we would love to hear from you. You can share your thoughts via one of the links above, or, if you purchased the book online, reviews can be posted on the vendor's website.

Thank you!